**"We're driving away from the safe house,"
Ayla said.**

"Yes, I'm aware of that." The last thing he needed was her nitpicking his every move.

"You agree we're in danger?"

Before Chance replied, Ayla reached for his cell phone and called 911 reporting the vehicle.

"Don't shoot yet," Chance warned. "It could be a hot rod trying to pass us." His hesitation came from years of facing public scrutiny as law enforcement. A premature reaction could result in a bad outcome.

"Yeah right." Ayla's tone was thick with sarcasm as she positioned in the seat.

"Destiny, down!"

The dog quickly disappeared into her kennel and Chance slid the divider closed.

Ayla rolled down her window.

"What're you doing?" Her take-charge personality threw Chance, but he had no time to process the information before the massive push bar on the truck's grille roared into his rearview mirror.

A slam from behind thrust them forward, and the pickup fishtailed.

Sharee Stover is a Colorado native transplanted to Nebraska, where she lives with her husband, three children and two dogs. Her mother instilled in her a love of books before Sharee could read, along with the promise "if you can read, you can do anything." When she's not writing, she enjoys time with her family, long walks with her obnoxiously lovable German shepherd and crocheting. Find her at shareestover.com or on Twitter, @shareestover.

Books by Sharee Stover

Love Inspired Suspense

Secret Past
Silent Night Suspect
Untraceable Evidence
Grave Christmas Secrets
Cold Case Trail
Tracking Concealed Evidence
Framing the Marshal
Defending the Witness

Visit the Author Profile page at LoveInspired.com.

DEFENDING THE WITNESS

SHAREE STOVER

LOVE INSPIRED SUSPENSE
INSPIRATIONAL ROMANCE

LOVE INSPIRED® SUSPENSE
INSPIRATIONAL ROMANCE

Recycling programs
for this product may
not exist in your area.

ISBN-13: 978-1-335-59753-3

Defending the Witness

Copyright © 2023 by Sharee Stover

For questions and comments about the quality of this book, please contact us
at CustomerService@Harlequin.com.

Love Inspired
22 Adelaide St. West, 41st Floor
Toronto, Ontario M5H 4E3, Canada
www.LoveInspired.com

Printed in U.S.A.

In the multitude of my thoughts within me
thy comforts delight my soul.
—*Psalm* 94:19

All glory and honor to Jesus Christ, my Redeemer.

Without the support of my wonderful husband and children, my dream of writing would've been impossible. Thank you for your love and encouragement.

Acknowledgments:

Thank you to the real Marissa and her equine friends who helped make the Walsh Horse Ranch come alive.

ONE

Ayla DuPree stood prepared to fire with both arms extended, aiming her SF-12 Glock at the target. Though Deputy US Marshal Ezra Pullman wasn't present, his instructions replayed in her mind. *Take the kill shot.*

A warm autumn breeze kissed her neck, fluttering her long auburn hair, and the tall grass swayed around her legs. Twilight had fallen, casting shadows over the Nebraska cornfields and cow pastures. Crickets chirruped in chorus with cicadas, and the last birdsongs ushered in the night.

"Be the wave maker," Ayla whispered to herself, and then she inhaled and held a fortifying breath. Steadying her hand, she pulled the trigger.

A blast ruptured the peaceful setting and penetrated the target. Ezra had taught her well.

She lowered the weapon. Satisfaction at her impeccable shot mingled with sadness that no one else was around to see it. Twenty miles away, the residents of small-town Minden remained oblivious to the witness in the safe house, completing Ezra's intention of hiding her there.

Ayla's fear of guns had morphed into respect and confidence for the power they provided in her quest to stay alive, but she never relished the idea of using one on another human being. She holstered the weapon and trailed through the makeshift training area where she'd spent the last six months learning hand-to-hand combat, firearms and other survival skills. In that time, Myles Sutler and the EastSide7 gang hadn't shown their criminal faces, adding to Ayla's belief that she didn't need WitSec protection.

As though she'd spoken the words aloud, Ezra's voice again interrupted her thoughts. *Preparation is part of the battle. You don't get ready for the fight in the thick of it.*

The last slivers of sunlight rested on the horizon. Ayla moved closer, inspecting the gelatin ballistics training mannequin she'd nicknamed George sitting on the tree stump. "I suppose that's enough practice for today." A wave of loneliness passed over Ayla. "How pathetic am I? I'm talking to a mannequin. No offense, George."

Her outdoor accompaniment resumed with the night insects' songs, and somewhere in the distance, a cow mooed.

"Time to go." Ayla hefted the mannequin with an *oomph* and carried it to the antiquated barn adjacent to the training space. Despite the worn exterior, the solid structure housed a newer-model SUV. Ayla placed George on the front passenger seat per Ezra's text message instructions and exited the barn, spotting headlights bouncing on the horizon.

Ezra was right on time.

Ayla hurried up the hill to the house just as her cell phone chimed. Ezra. Confused, she glanced again at the lights in the distance. Why was he calling when he was so close? "Worried I ran away?" she answered teasingly. She entered the front door and watched the vehicle drawing closer.

"Ayla, they're coming! Drive to the location circled on the map in the console."

She registered the urgency in his voice, and confusion set in. "What about you?"

"Don't wait for me."

"But you're almost here. I see your car."

"What? No! Go, Ayla! I've called for backup. I'm on my way, but I'm at least twenty minutes out."

Realization tackled her. It wasn't Ezra coming up the hill.

"Get out of there!"

Without responding, Ayla shoved the phone into her pocket and sprinted from the house. Her footfalls pounded against the ground as she aimed for the barn. Behind her, doors slammed, and the sound of men's voices reached her.

Ayla glanced over her shoulder, spotting a man on the porch. He swung his arm, and Ayla bolted forward just as an explosion rocked the atmosphere.

She face-planted on the hard earth, air whooshing from her lungs. Ayla groaned, her ears ringing and her body limp from the impact. *No time. Get up.* She pushed up and twisted around.

Orange and red flames stretched into the night sky, consuming the house, and heat radiated from the structure. No sign of the men. Had they gone? Was it over?

In reply to her unspoken questions, gunshots pelted the dirt beside her. Ayla wrapped her arms over her head, simultaneously jumping to her feet and sprinting for the barn's open door.

She slid behind the wheel of the SUV, glancing to her right, and screamed at the presence riding shotgun.

George sat in the passenger seat.

Recognition coursed through her, and with shaking hands, she attempted to insert the key into the ignition, missing several times before successfully starting the engine.

She shifted into Drive, leaving the headlights off, and barreled out of the barn, speeding through the pasture.

Bullets struck the vehicle, shattering the passenger window but never reaching her. "Thanks, George," she mumbled, grateful the mannequin took the hits.

Lights bounced in her rearview mirror, the attackers in pursuit.

Ayla mashed the pedal to the floor, bounding over the rutted tracks left by tractors, then turned right.

An enormous farm combine parked near a Y in the road caught her eye, and she drove toward it, seeking cover. She pulled forward and exhaled as the lights moved in the opposite direction.

Perfect.

After several minutes, Ayla pulled out from her hiding spot. She wasted no time merging onto the county highway but waited to turn on the headlights until she was certain no one followed.

Miles of country passed her window, and she noticed a dense grove beside a Quonset hut. The location provided the optimal opportunity to pull over and check the map Ezra had mentioned. Once parked behind the steel building, she tried calling Ezra's phone, but the line went straight to voice mail. She withdrew a paper map from the console and studied it, using a pen flashlight from the glove box.

She mentally calculated the time and distance to the location Ezra had circled near Gavin's Point Dam. At least a three-hour drive via major highways, but the fastest route might prove unwise. Instead, she mapped an alternative way, taking country roads, veering off, then intermittently changing direction. It increased the drive time but provided opportunities to lose a tail should one occur.

Or should she wait for Ezra?

Once more, Ayla accepted she was on her own. She'd love to drive south to Texas where her mother and Boyd, her brother, had moved four years prior due to Mama's health issues. Boyd's teenage naivete and her mother's fragile condition made it impossible for Ayla to visit, and Ayla's presence might endanger them if EastSide7 followed her.

She folded the map and tucked it inside her jean jacket pocket before calling Ezra again.

It rang three times before a man said, "Hello, Ayla. Your friend Ezra is dead. And you're next."

She gasped and threw the phone out the window. She wouldn't give Myles Sutler or his EastSide7 cronies a way to track her. She shifted into gear and headed north.

Ayla took random turns onto country roads, all the while searching for signs of trailing vehicles. The lengthy drive gave her time to ponder everything that had happened in the last six months. The thoughts provided no reassurance—rather they bred more questions than answers. Trust was a precious commodity, especially after witnessing RJ's murder at the hands of Myles Sutler, leader of EastSide7.

Her thoughts traveled to RJ, her father's dearest friend whom she'd trusted since childhood. He and his wife, Octavia, had stepped into the roles of uncle and aunt respectively, helping Ayla's mother after her father's death. RJ had hired Ayla as his paralegal and assistant in Des Moines. When her mother moved with Boyd to start a new life in Texas—a decision Ayla totally supported, wanting them both to be happy—RJ and Octavia had remained close to Ayla. In all of that, she'd not doubted RJ's integrity...until it was too late.

Ezra had earned her trust over time, but unlike her father and RJ, he didn't play games or sugarcoat things. Yet, a single phone conversation she'd eavesdropped on a few days prior bounced to the forefront of her mind. Ezra had mentioned "the list." Two normal, ordinary words. Words she'd heard before. Spoken together, they had preceded RJ's death and plunged her into WitSec.

When Ayla spotted the sign depicting Crofton twenty miles ahead, she exhaled relief. She turned onto a county minimum maintenance road, determined to stay off the main highway. A glance at the dashboard clock revealed it was nearing midnight, and she hadn't passed another vehicle for twenty minutes at least. Headlights appeared from the single-lane road on the left, evaporating her relief and making the hair rise on her neck. She sucked in a breath, eyes fixed on the rearview mirror as the dark sedan slid behind her.

Had Myles tracked her?

Ayla took the next available turn, then accelerated and merged onto Highway 81, passing a semitruck. The car imitated her move.

Ayla's chest constricted.

She increased her speed, welcoming the idea of a cop pulling her over. At least then she'd have backup.

The driver kept up, and just when Ayla accepted her future demise, he deviated off the highway and trekked east. Ayla wasn't convinced he'd stay gone, so she took the next right, down a dirt road, cresting a hill, onto Highway 12.

She'd take a detour over Gavin's Point Dam into South Dakota, then circle back across the river to the Nebraska cabin Ezra had denoted on the map. Satisfied with her new plan, she headed for Highway 121.

Ayla slowed as she rounded Crest Road. The dam's connected power plant impeded the view of the single-lane road bridging the two states over the Missouri River and Lewis and Clark Lake. A stoplight allowed each side to pass safely, but sitting still wasn't beneficial, and her anxiety peaked. Ayla inched around the enormous structure and started across, praying no one came from the other side at the same time.

She'd made it to the center of the road when bright headlights illuminated, forcing her to avert her eyes. Ayla slammed on the brakes, trapped. The sedan didn't move, but it prohibited her escape. She tapped her jean pocket and realized she must have dropped the Glock running from the house. Ayla ducked down in the seat, averting her eyes, and ran her hand along the undersides in search of a weapon. *Please, let there be a gun.* Her fingers grazed something cold, and she withdrew the object.

A crowbar.

She didn't want to get close enough to the shooters to swing a crowbar, and that was no match for the firepower they brought.

Now what?

Images of her childhood burst from her memory. She recalled boys in the neighborhood building bike ramps and launching themselves into the air. If she gained the necessary momentum, would the SUV spring off the shooter's car? Worst-case scenario, she'd cause a head-on collision.

She flipped on her bright headlights, dazing the shooters, just as they'd done to her.

Gunshots blasted, shattering the windshield.

With her foot on the brake, Ayla flung open the driver's door.

More gunfire pinged off the SUV.

She wedged the crowbar against the gas pedal, then she launched herself out of the vehicle.

Ayla slammed hard into the guardrail.

The SUV sped forward, its door swinging wildly. The shooters continued blasting away.

Ayla dived off the dam just as a flash of lightning splintered across the sky.

* * *

"We have a body!"

"It's gruesome. Incomplete."

The rescue workers' grisly announcements snapped Deputy US Marshal Chance Tavalla to attention. He slammed his truck door and tugged on his baseball cap, then secured his German shepherd's tracking harness. "Heel." She fell into step beside him, and they approached a hulking Nebraska state trooper, supervising the men extracting the body from the river.

"Deputy US Marshal Chance Tavalla, and this is K-9 Destiny." Chance extended his hand.

"Lieutenant Nathan Lassiter." He returned the handshake. "We're thankful for your help. Beckham Walsh speaks highly of you."

The words threw him, considering Walsh had appeared disinterested in Chance as the newest member of the Heartland Fugitive Task Force. "We'll do everything we can to help," he assured the lieutenant.

The crime scene juxtaposed the picturesque landscape, where an eagle soared against soft pastels painting the morning sky. Multiple law enforcement vehicles and personnel marred the rocky shoreline beside Gavin's Point Dam. A tow truck growled as it winched Ezra Pullman's SUV from the water.

They reached the river's edge, and Chance saw what appeared to be a human torso wedged between the massive red rocks.

The first rescue worker turned, wearing a sheepish expression. "Sorry, I overreacted."

Chance stifled a grin, recognizing the expensive ballistics training mannequin. What was it doing here?

Lassiter offered the kid a pat on the shoulder. "I prefer that to a delayed response. With the limited lighting and position, no wonder you thought it was a human. Thankfully, this isn't a victim."

"One of our members is an ATF agent." Chance knelt and inspected the bullet-impacted gel. "She'll have the best resources for ballistics analysis."

"I'll ensure it gets to her first," Lassiter replied.

"Thank you." Chance typed a text message and snapped a picture, sending it to ATF agent Skyler Rios. His phone buzzed with her reply. On it.

The trio walked to where crew members and crime scene technicians documented the evidence. A tow truck worker winched the SUV onto his rig, and water poured from the vehicle. The passenger side window was gone. Had the mannequin fallen out?

Chance edged closer. Bullet holes pierced the exterior. Based on the physical damage, he surmised the nosedive off Gavin's Point Dam Road had ripped the driver's door from its hinges. Only one of the thirteen overflow doors stood open, funneling Lewis and Clark Lake into the Missouri River. The rest of the concrete base stood above the water, explaining the delay in the SUV's travels underwater.

"Where will you tow the vehicle?"

"We'll take it to the state lab for analysis," Lieutenant Lassiter said.

"Have you located any survivors?" Chance deliberately refrained from saying Ayla's name, anticipating the lieutenant's answer.

"None."

Ezra's notification of his compromised location came too late. He'd died before the Heartland Fugitive Task Force arrived, and his assigned witness, Ayla DuPree, was missing. The team hoped she'd escaped, tasking Chance and Destiny with finding her.

Lassiter glanced past him. "Dive teams will attempt

to sweep the river. However, be aware that's a long shot. They're reluctant to investigate too close to the dam because of the powerful undertow."

If Ayla had plunged into the water unconscious, she was already dead.

Chance's instinct said otherwise.

He surveyed the bordering forest. A thunderstorm had raged through the county the previous night. That complicated matters for Destiny, though he felt confident she'd sniff out Ayla's path.

"Sir, we'd like to canvass the area," Chance said—as a courtesy, since they didn't require the lieutenant's permission.

"Absolutely. Let me know if you need anything," Lassiter replied.

Chance led Destiny toward the steep incline, and they climbed to the road, pausing at skid marks and damage to the railing. Glass, metal and plastic, along with an array of bullet casings, littered the ground, confirming Chance's supposition that another vehicle was involved. Crime scene techs documented evidence with numbered yellow placards. If the other car belonged to EastSide7, the gang had ensured it was nowhere to be found.

"Seek." Chance offered Destiny the scent article preserved from Ayla's case file, and they started the search.

As they neared the center, Destiny paused, pacing beside the railing. She sat and barked twice.

Chance's heart drummed. A piece of denim hung snagged in the metal chain-link fence. *Score!* Ayla had been here.

Chance rewarded his partner with her favorite shark tug toy and praises. Then he leaned over the railing facing the lake and tried to picture the scene in his mind.

If EastSide7 had forced her vehicle off the road, had she jumped? The extensive distance to either shore made a water escape difficult, but not impossible. Additionally, the thick cover of trees on the Nebraska side offered excellent hiding places.

"Ayla DuPree, where are you?" He lifted his binoculars and swept the landscape, lingering on an object floating on the lake near a boat ramp.

"Sorry, girl. Time to work." Chance wrestled Destiny's toy from her and placed it in the largest pocket of his cargo pants.

They returned to his truck and loaded inside.

"What a mess." His K-9 poked her head through the divider, leaning on his shoulder. "We're supposed to find a fugitive witness without alerting anyone she's missing? This should be interesting."

Destiny emitted a *mrff*—a term Chance used to describe her muffled bark—of understanding. Ayla's case file sat beside him, but he'd studied it ad nauseam, easily recalling her picture from memory, along with the code words *wave maker*.

No denying the woman's beauty, but Chance's prior interactions with Ayla had left a bitter taste in his mouth. Her undisputed devotion to Judge RJ Warden had Chance questioning her scruples. However, based on the information he'd read, Ayla's deceased father and RJ were longtime friends. Regardless, years of law enforcement experience had developed Chance's ability to read people. His instincts and the few interactions he'd had with RJ left Chance with a disingenuous impression of the judge, though he'd never admit that as a new member of the Heartland Fugitive Task Force. He wouldn't appear anything other than enthusiastic about every assignment. But he and Destiny were fugitive trackers, not babysitters, so when they found Ayla, he'd pass her off to another team member for witness protection.

Chance shifted into gear and headed across the dam to the road that paralleled the lake. He drove to where he estimated the boat floated and parked in the wooded area away from traffic. Once he and Destiny had exited the vehicle, he said, "Ready to work?"

She gave an affirming *mrff* and wagged her tail. He trusted his partner's nose—a weapon to be reckoned with—and her impeccable track record.

"Let's find our witness." He again offered Destiny a long whiff of the scent article. "Seek."

She led Chance away from the road, into the forest area and down to the dock, where she alerted. The small fishing boat floated across from them. They continued along the shore, then moved into the woods.

An hour later, Chance's growing frustration had him debating whether to reassess the search. He watched the ground for signs of disturbance, but leaves, sticks and rocks covered the earth, concealing depressions.

Suddenly, Destiny took off like a shot down a valley, forcing Chance to jog. She shifted direction and headed across a gravel road into a wooded area. He ducked low-hanging branches, tromping over brambles. His boots crunched the pine needles, and leaves slapped his face and arms.

Destiny moved faster toward a strange lean-to. *Score!* She'd found Ayla.

Chance's elation evaporated at the empty shelter. He grumbled and looked closer. A dent in the ground indicated a possible visitor, gone now. "So close."

Ignoring him, Destiny sniffed the exterior, then barked and dashed from the lean-to and crested a hill. An old tire painted with the threat Trespassers Will Be Shot hung on an iron cattle gate. Since Destiny couldn't read, she ignored the warning and lunged forward.

Sunlight glimmered off something in the distance. The green metal roof of a log cabin nestled deep within the foliage that concealed the structure. A shadowed figure stood at the door, turning at their approach, then bolting around the back side of the cabin.

Destiny strained against her leash, nearly yanking Chance's arm out of the socket. They pursued through downed pines that forced them to slow and search among the debris. Destiny aimed for a monstrous maple hovering at the valley edge. She barked twice, then sat near a hollowed-out trunk.

"Good job!" Chance praised, catching up. Destiny moved obediently to his side. "Down."

She dropped to a sit, and he released the leash, freeing his hand to withdraw his weapon. He inched toward the tree, gaining a better look. Gun trained, he warned, "US Marshal. Come out slowly with your hands up."

No response.

Chance repeated the order, louder, "Come out or I'll send my dog in."

"Leave me alone," a female voice pleaded.

"Now."

Dirt crunched from inside the tree before a hand first emerged. In painfully slow acknowledgment, the woman unfolded herself from the space and crawled out. Soft tendrils in coordinating hues of auburn and gold hung loose, concealing her face. She turned her head to the side, catching sight of Destiny, and froze in place.

"Get to your feet slowly. Don't make any sudden movements," Chance instructed.

"Um. Will the dog attack me?"

"Not unless I tell her to."

With her hands in the air, the woman looked up, her striking emerald eyes colliding with his.

Ayla DuPree. He'd found her.

Rather, Destiny had.

"Is it leashed?" Ayla focused on his partner.

"You don't have to be afraid."

"Please. Give me a little room."

Chance exhaled and holstered his gun, gathering Destiny's leash and pulling her closer next to him. "There." He took two steps back. "Ayla, I'm—"

Without warning, Ayla burst from the space, holding a rope. She whipped it downward.

A zipping sound drew Chance's attention, and he looked up just as something snagged his feet, yanking him and Destiny into the air. The distinct stench of fish and the coarse ropes confirmed they were bound in a fishing net.

They swung, suspended from the maple tree. Destiny whimpered, trying to get a foothold and failing as her paws slipped through the netting.

"Ayla! Wait!" She ignored Chance's command and sprinted toward the forest.

TWO

Ayla sprinted at the edge of the foothill, pumping her arms to increase her pace. She sent up a silent prayer of thanks for finding the net in the boat several hours before. Once more, Ezra's training had proven beneficial, but she'd only bought herself a tiny window of time. She'd never outrun the dog if they escaped the net. Ezra's words floated on the breeze. *Your enemy seeks to eliminate you. Never assume they'll offer mercy.*

Sharp, piercing barks echoed, driving a chill through Ayla. She scoured the landscape for a hiding place, spotting the man and canine in her peripheral vision.

She gasped and lunged to the side, zigzagging between the trees. He wasn't shooting at her yet, and she prayed he'd lose sight of her.

The sliver of a creek in the next valley emerged in her view. The dog couldn't trace her in the water. Desperation fueled Ayla, and she sprinted uphill.

Glancing over her shoulder was her mistake.

A hard body tackled her from the side, and his arms wrapped tightly around her torso. "Ayla!"

She refused to surrender, twisting to break free of his hold. Ayla drove her foot backward, striking his knee. He yelled out but didn't release her. They stumbled in an awkward dance before tumbling down the hill in a flurry of dirt, leaves and debris.

When they finally stopped, Ayla gasped, still partially strapped in his embrace, and fought to regain her bearings. She sucked in a breath, yanked back her arm simultaneously and drove her elbow into the man's face.

He growled and, in a lightning-fast countermove, tightened his hold, pinning her arms tightly against her sides again and wrapping his legs around hers. Trapped in his stranglehold, she wriggled and screamed.

"Wave maker. Wave maker!"

At the code words, Ayla stilled. "What?" She panted.

"Wave maker." His breath was hot against her ear. "My name is Deputy US Marshal Chance Tavalla. I'm here to help you."

Like snowflakes in a blizzard, his reply fluttered for a place to land. Adrenaline collided with Ayla's emotions and exertion. "Let go of me!"

"Not yet."

The late-night escape from EastSide7 had left her exhausted, hungry and confused. "Let go of me," she repeated, resisting him.

"Ayla DuPree, I will not hurt you." His chest rose and fell with heavy breathing. "I'll release my hold once you stop fighting me. I'm here to help you."

"Okay," she mumbled, contemplating her next move and barely hearing his words. If she could somehow get away, dodge him, then run to the cabin...

"Destiny!" She heard a shuffling in the distance, then the beautiful German shepherd appeared beside them. As if sensing Ayla's mental debate, the man said, "Don't try it or I will send my dog after you. And believe me, you won't like that."

Ayla glanced at the animal's sharp, shiny white teeth and relented. "Fine."

The man released his hold and shifted back, getting to his feet. His black baseball cap shadowed his face, and his ballistic vest, worn over a short-sleeved black T-shirt, displayed the US Marshal star. He wore coffee-colored cargo pants and combat boots. If nothing else, he looked the part. He fisted his hand, bent at the elbow, and in a downward motion, signaled a silent command.

Ayla sucked in a breath, frozen in place.

The animal immediately dropped to a sphinx pose, panting softly.

"Is it okay to move?" she whispered, gaze fixated on the creature.

The marshal gave a slight nod. "Slowly."

Ayla shifted to sit.

The rising sun silhouetted him. He extended a hand, and she responded with a wary glance, shielding her eyes. "Say it again."

"What?"

"The code."

"Wave maker." Impatience flickered in his tone.

The phrase she and Ezra had established should something separate them. A play on words for her situation since she'd made enormous waves that developed into a tsunami, forcing her to run for her life after witnessing Judge RJ Warden's murder.

Myles Sutler and EastSide7 would do anything to keep her from testifying.

Ezra's death was proof. Her heart hitched at the thought of the kind man's demise.

All because of her.

She took the proffered hand and stood, then dusted off her jeans. "Chance, you said?"

"Yes."

"Were you a friend of his?"

When he didn't immediately answer, Ayla's pulse increased. Had she made a terminal mistake? Was this man a marshal? He didn't radio to anyone. Where were the rest of the cops? Her eyes darted, searching for others. They appeared to be alone. Would he kill her here? What should she do? She glanced again at the dog.

Finally, he responded. "Yes, I knew Ezra very well."

Past tense.

The single word erased any lingering hope that Ezra had survived and whoever answered his phone the night before had simply lied.

She swallowed hard.

"How did you find me?" She glanced at the shepherd. "I mean, obviously he did—"

"*She.* Meet K-9 Destiny. Scent tracking and apprehension expert extraordinaire."

At her name, the shepherd's thick tail wagged, and she tilted her head, her large triangular ears perked.

"Be grateful she doesn't hold a grudge. She's not used to escaping fishing nets."

Ayla cringed. "I thought you were with EastSide7." She looked down.

"The move was ingenious. When my eyes stop watering and I can breathe out of my nose, I'll ask how you did it."

"Sorry about that elbow to your face." A smile tugged at Ayla's lips; she was intrigued but apprehensive. "Pleased to meet you, Destiny. Wait." Her gaze bounced between the team. "Chance and Destiny? For real?"

He shrugged. "The department named her before partnering us."

"Cute." Ayla shifted from one foot to another. "How'd

you get out of the fishing net?" Had she failed to secure it correctly?

"Oh, thanks for reminding me." Chance reached into the lower right pocket of his cargo pants and withdrew a Leatherman knife that he tucked behind his back. "I always have extra resources."

"You keep a knife with you?"

"Several."

He didn't offer to show her the locations of the others. What other provisions had Chance hidden?

"I could handcuff you, but it'll make trekking this rough terrain difficult. Instead, I'll warn you not to run." His serious, no-nonsense tone spoke volumes. "Before we go any farther, be aware that Destiny makes no distinction. If you take off, I will let her assume you're the target."

"Point made." Ayla redirected the conversation. "You didn't answer my question. We're a long way from the safe house. How did you find me here?" She gestured toward the open space filled with trees and hills.

"Ezra's vehicle antitheft software—something he should've disabled but hadn't—listed Gavin's Point Dam as the last known location. I followed the rest of the clues. The mess of a crime scene, and the boat you left floating aimlessly in the middle of Lewis and Clark Lake. I'm guessing that's where you got the net you used on us?"

"Yeah. Ezra taught me how to make the trap." Sadness settled on Ayla's shoulders at the mention of her handler. She refocused her thoughts on how the dog had found her and turned in what she assumed was the direction of the dam's location, though the landscape blocked her view. "That's a long way."

"Destiny's got skills," he replied without expounding. His expression sobered. "How did *you* get here?"

"I dived off the dam and swam."

He quirked a disbelieving brow. "No, really. How did you end up so far from the SUV?"

"I told you, I swam," she answered, refusing to elaborate. Two could play that game.

"Impressive."

Ayla shrugged. "Fear and adrenaline are effective motivators." And years of her efforts on the local swim team had paid off. Her mother would be proud. If she lived to tell her about it someday.

"Do you have any injuries?" Chance swiped at his nose for emphasis.

"Again, sorry about that." Ayla gestured to his face.

"It was a solid hit. Kudos." He lifted his phone. "Great. No reception." Pocketing the device, he asked, "Besides Olympic swimming and MMA fighting skills, is there anything else you need to share?"

She forced away a grin. "Not really."

"This time you didn't answer my question. Were you injured?" He seemed to survey her from beneath the ball cap.

Ayla crossed her arms and looked down at her crusty jeans, sand- and dirt-covered shoes, and ripped jean jacket, aware of her disheveled appearance. She attempted to dust them off but only managed to further smear the fabric. "No. What led you to me?"

"Nebraska State Patrol identified Ezra's vehicle with his alias registration," Chance said.

"It worked," she proclaimed with satisfaction.

"Beg your pardon?"

"I wedged a crowbar on the gas pedal, hoping the SUV kept going." She faced him with a smile. "The shooters trapped me on the dam, but when we escaped the safe house, George took most of the hits."

That got Chance's attention. "George? There's a victim?"

"No. The gelatin ballistic mannequin."

A grin crossed his lips, enhancing his handsome features. "I see. George got stuck in the rocks after the SUV nosedived off the dam. He's fine and on the way to the state lab for ballistics analysis."

"George saved my life." Ayla cocked her head to the right. "I didn't have many options."

"Ezra taught you well. That was ingenious and brave." The compliment came unbidden.

Or foolish, because it left her stranded and faced with whether to trust this stranger, claiming to be a marshal to the rescue. "Thanks."

Chance moved closer, tipping up the end of the ball cap and revealing his face. Ayla's heart stuttered at his handsome features until recognition overtook her response. "Sergeant Scrutiny?" As soon as the private nickname escaped her lips, Ayla longed to inhale it in again. Had she said that aloud?

Yep. Based on his peaked brows and frown, she had.

Defiance overcame embarrassment. Well, he deserved it. She and Judge RJ had referred to him as Sergeant Scrutiny so often she'd forgotten Chance's real name. They'd had a few unpleasant interactions, and both RJ and Chance hadn't hidden their opinions of one another. As RJ's paralegal and assistant, Ayla had defended her boss and mentor. That was before she'd found the evidence that changed her world and jolted her trust shield higher than ever. The documents she'd never confronted RJ with before his death.

"I recognize you from the courthouse." A weak attempt at covering her faux pas, but for the moment, it'd have to do.

"Yeah, we've met," he snapped, gathering the dog's leash. "We need to get back to my team." He paused, glancing up at the hill. "Why were you at that cabin?"

At his reminder, Ayla took the lead. "That's where Ezra told me to go."

Chance and Destiny hurried beside her. "How long were you out here?"

"Forever." She sighed. "I dived off the dam a little after midnight and kept moving, setting traps along the way in case the gang followed me." Sheepishly, she admitted, "I must've dozed off. I got to the cabin just as I heard you talking to Destiny." She quickened her pace through the trees. "The door's locked, though."

"Easy fix." Chance moved ahead of her, which she preferred to facing him.

Handsome didn't touch Chance Tavalla. The black T-shirt and ballistic vest outlined his muscular form, and his cerulean-blue eyes contrasted with his dark hair.

For all the attraction Chance's good looks awakened, his personality brought out the worst in Ayla every time they'd interacted at the courthouse. RJ had never spoken an approving word about Sergeant Scrutiny, especially because the marshal questioned any case he'd worked under RJ's appointment.

Considering the developments of the past six months, Ayla pondered if she'd misjudged Chance. If so, she owed him a sincere apology.

Later. He had a job to do, and she wanted to go somewhere safe.

Ayla jogged to catch up. "I'm sorry. I shouldn't have said that."

"I've been called worse." He gave her a sideways grin that sent warmth radiating up her neck. "I understand loyalty to your bully of a boss, though he and I didn't see eye to eye on much of anything. Guess you're aware of that."

Ayla stiffened at the reminder. She'd spent her whole life adoring RJ, so her first reaction—to defend him—confused her emotions. "You said we're going to your team?"

she asked, changing the subject. "What's that mean? Another safe house? Are you my new handler?"

"No way." Chance snorted. "I'll pass you off to my commander and he'll decide what the next steps are. Destiny and I are fugitive trackers."

"I am not a fugitive," Ayla argued.

"You are as far as I'm concerned."

This was one infuriating man. And she needed answers. "Wait." She placed a hand on his arm, the muscles tensing beneath her hold. Ayla jerked back. "How did Myles and his gang find me in the safe house? And what happened to Ezra?"

Chance faced her. "Ezra was on his way to meet you when Sutler, or one of his cronies, ambushed him on the road. He believed they'd compromised your location."

"He called and told me to leave. I should've waited."

"There's nothing you could've done. He died instantly." He touched her shoulder gently, and she shrugged away from him.

Why did people think that was a comfort?

Ayla climbed the two wooden steps to the cabin door and reached for the knob. Chance withdrew a small tool from a vest pocket and inserted it into the lock. A click sounded, and the door opened. "Wait here until I clear the interior."

She leaned against the porch railing as Destiny and Chance entered. They returned within a minute. "It's good."

Ayla strolled through the quaint, sparsely decorated cabin with a tan-and-red-checkered love seat centered across from a wood-burning stove. Two chairs and a small table were shoved against the far wall beside a kitchenette. To the left, a doorway revealed a compact bathroom with a standup shower, and the bedroom opposite held a double bed and lamp. Clean, but not appropriate or equipped for more than one person. How had Ezra figured they'd stay here?

Ayla pulled out the crunchy, wrinkled mess of a map and confirmed they were in the right place.

Chance moved closer. "Where'd you get that?"

"From Ezra. He told me to come here." She pointed to the spot, now smeared.

Chance withdrew his phone and snapped a picture. "Before I call my team, is there anything else you can tell me about last night?"

"Weren't you aware of the new location? Isn't that something Ezra would've shared with you?"

An expression she couldn't quite explain crossed his face, and he frowned. "How long had you known about the cabin?"

"He told me yesterday morning." A sudden nervousness had Ayla stiffening. Ezra's reminder that *not everything is as it seems* hovered in her mind. He wasn't spontaneous. He'd planned for them to leave, anticipating the attack.

Was Chance trustworthy? Her heart pounded in her throat, heavy and fearful.

He stepped forward and Ayla backed up, bumping into the sofa.

"What?" He glanced over his shoulder.

"Um, nothing." She hated the tremor in her voice. "I need to use the bathroom." Ayla scurried to the confined space and closed the door behind her. *Lord, grant me wisdom. I've foolishly trusted people before. If Chance is out to harm me, give me a way of escape.*

Two raps. "Ayla, are you okay?"

Destiny whined, a high-pitched whistle that resembled a plea.

"Coming." Ayla turned on the faucet and splashed the

cool water on her face. In her mirrored reflection, she noticed a suspicious knot in the log wall behind her. Running her hands over the spot, she discovered a cabinet door. She tugged, and when it opened, she gasped at the arsenal of hidden weapons.

"Ayla. What's going on?" Chance's muffled voice interrupted her perusal.

"I'll be out in a second." She reached for the Beretta Pico, familiar with handling the small pistol while in training. Once she ensured it contained ammunition, she slipped it into the inside pocket of her jean jacket and softly closed the cabinet.

When she exited the bathroom, Chance stood in the narrow hallway, arms crossed over his chest and feet shoulder width apart. His commanding presence and impressive stature consumed the space. "Tried to escape and realized there's no window?"

Ayla gave a nervous laugh. "Whatever."

"Okay, then spill."

"What?" The weight of the gun hung heavy on her conscience.

"We're committed to keeping you safe." He gestured toward Destiny sitting beside him. "Honesty is key."

"I understand," Ayla replied.

"You have no reason to trust me, but I assure you Ezra and I work for the same side of justice."

That's what I'm worried about. "Sure." She moved past him, breaking eye contact and contemplating her options. She couldn't outrun Destiny.

"Let's talk about the events that led to your escape so I can update my team."

She dropped onto the love seat. Her misplaced trust had proven detrimental before, thrusting her into her current predicament.

Her gaze darted to the door where Chance had repositioned, blocking her getaway. As if sensing her unease, Destiny moved closer to Ayla, tilting her head in a silent conversation and absorbing Ayla into the dark pools of her gentle eyes. "Is it okay to pet her?"

"Sure, just move slowly and let her sniff your hands first."

Panic rose in Ayla's chest. Would the dog smell the gun?

Chance crossed the room and knelt beside Destiny, stroking her neck and head. "She always seems to know what I'm thinking," he said. "And she's a superb judge of character."

Fabulous. Guilt and apprehension weighed on Ayla. Destiny shifted, resting her chin on Ayla's lap with a sigh. The tension dissipated. The dog hadn't alerted.

"So," Chance said, interrupting her thoughts, "have you had the gun this entire time?"

Ayla's eyes froze on his cerulean gaze. "Did Destiny tell you?"

"No. You did." Chance chuckled and gestured to Ayla.

The pistol peeked from her pocket. She glanced down and grimaced. "Oh."

"Are you trained to use it?"

Was that a challenge? She straightened. "Yes."

He flashed a smile. "Good. If it makes you feel safer to have your own weapon, hold on to it."

She blinked, confused. Wasn't he going to take it away? Tie her to a chair or something? "I don't know who to trust," she blurted.

"You trusted me."

"I'm here because you said the code word and your dog would outrun me effortlessly," Ayla corrected. "Don't mistake that for trust."

"You're right. My bad." His expression softened. "After

everything you've endured, I understand your apprehension. I just hope you'll see Destiny and me as friends, not foes."

Ayla bowed her head, meeting Destiny's gentle stare. She reached out, allowing the dog to sniff her hand. At Chance's affirming nod, she stroked the animal's dark fur. "I was doing a training exercise with George." She explained everything that had happened prior to Destiny finding her in the hollowed-out tree. "If EastSide7 compromised our location, that means something is wrong with *your* system."

"No argument there." He stood and ran a hand over his head, drawing Ayla's attention to the muscled bicep peeking from his T-shirt sleeve.

She averted her eyes.

"What you're telling me isn't lining up with Ezra's latest update."

"What aren't you saying?"

Destiny lay at her feet, and soft breaths indicated she'd fallen asleep.

"Did you see any signs or have concerns Ezra was working with Myles Sutler?" Chance pressed.

"No, Ezra—" Ayla hesitated, unsure whether to share more. Images of her handler helping and training her conflicted with doubts about his trustworthiness. "I don't know what to believe. Do you think he was in cahoots with them?"

"My initial reaction is no, but I'm not dismissing anything right now."

Chance wasn't ignoring the possibilities for the sake of the brotherhood, and he valued her concerns. His confusion at the information offered her reassurance. He hadn't taken away the gun or appeared threatened by her possessing it. Yet her mind circled in a loop of uncertainty.

"My team is the best, and once I've secured you in their care, you'll be safe." Without another word, he lifted his cell phone and made a call. He hovered near the door, then paced between the sofa and kitchenette.

Ayla, too, strode the confined, musty room while eavesdropping on his conversation.

"Yes, sir." A pause. "Correct. Sutler and his cronies traced her to the dam." He relayed the information Ayla had shared, word for word.

Impressive.

"That is my focus. Agreed."

She moved to the door. Destiny remained dozing, then quirked a furry brow in her direction as if reminding Ayla she was monitoring her movements. She smiled at the dog in reply.

"Miss DuPree should transition into the team's care." A pause. "With all due respect, Destiny and I are skilled fugitive hunters, not babysitters."

Ayla's head jerked up at the harsh words.

Chance rolled his eyes, apparently oblivious to the offensive statement's effect on her. "Yes, sir. Understood."

"I need air," she said aloud, reminding him of her presence.

He glanced up and nodded. *Leave the door open*, he mouthed.

Ayla stepped out onto the wooden porch. Why had Chance's comment stung? Because until she'd witnessed RJ's murder, she'd been independent. Now she was a burden.

She inhaled, absorbing the oxygen like caffeine to her soul, and surveyed the vast landscape. Serene rolling hills and tall trees decorated in fall splendor spanned her view. The crystal-clear water of Lewis and Clark Lake glistened in the distance. The scents of pine and wood wafted on the soft breeze.

This was where Ezra wanted her, but why? Was it the backup or next-in-line plan? Or had he told her to come here, intending to hand her over to Myles Sutler?

Chance's voice behind her carried in a low tone, but her ears worked like radar, taking in the one-sided conversation. "We'll head back to the satellite location to complete Miss DuPree's transfer."

Ayla sucked in a breath. Why was the thought of Chance handing her over morphing into fear? She barely knew him. She gripped the railing and pondered their earlier discussion, lingering on Chance's apparent confusion that Ezra had died defending her. He'd assumed she'd escaped the house before Myles had found her. How? He'd never answered that question. She pivoted, studying Chance. He paced between the door and the kitchenette, one hand holding the phone against his ear. Ayla stepped forward, hovering in the doorway, then she returned to the porch.

Could she trust him? If not, what was she supposed to do? Wait until night and take all the weapons from the bathroom and escape? Right. That wouldn't work with a German shepherd bodyguard.

As if responding to her thoughts, Destiny bolted from the house, barking, and ran in front of Ayla. "Um, Chance?"

The animal barked again, and Ayla took a step backward toward the cabin. She glanced over her shoulder. "Chance."

Without warning, Destiny barreled into her, shoving Ayla through the door. She landed on her behind with a thud, colliding with the love seat.

"Hey!" Ayla's protest died at the whizzing past her ear and the bullet that impaled the love seat beside her head.

THREE

Chance dived to slam the door shut, simultaneously yanking his gun from the holster. "Stay down and move behind the love seat!" To Destiny he ordered, "Down!"

The dog dropped into a crawl position, and Chance motioned for her to go to Ayla. With a reluctant glance and a whine, she obeyed. The two shifted out of sight.

Back flat against the wall beside the door, Chance peered out the corner of the window. Another shot whizzed past, narrowly missing his cheek as it ripped through the checkered curtain and shattered the glass. "Sniper," he mumbled.

"What do we do?" Ayla asked.

"One shooter, so he can't be in two places at once. I'll cover you and catch up. You take Destiny and go out the bedroom window. Head into the forest."

"No way. I'm not going alone. Ezra tried that and died."

Rapid fire pelted the log walls.

The sniper was growing impatient.

"I'm open to suggestions, but we need a distraction." Chance scanned the cabin for anything viable and came up empty.

"Bathroom. Now!" Ayla appeared on the floor beside the sofa in an army crawl.

"No!"

She ignored Chance, making her way to the hallway. He followed suit, motioning Destiny to do the same, and they trailed Ayla to the bathroom.

A firestorm of gunshots continued to riddle the cabin. Huddled inside the confining and windowless space, Ayla slammed the door shut.

"I don't think hiding is the solution," Chance said sarcastically, scouring his mind for an escape plan.

Ayla slid her hands along the wall, pausing at a knot in the wood, and tugged, revealing a cabinet. "Does this help?"

Chance stepped forward, his gaze roving the weapons arsenal. "Diversion covered." He snagged the Glock and an automatic rifle, then passed the remaining ammunition to Ayla.

The shooting ceased, leaving an eerie silence.

"He's coming in," Chance said. "Bedroom."

They dashed across the narrow hallway into the bedroom, facing the back side of the cabin. Chance tugged open the window. "Go. I'll catch up."

Ayla climbed out first, and he handed over Destiny's leash before hoisting the dog through. He turned and hurried out of the room, skidding to a halt at the shadow stretched along the floor.

Chance peered around the corner and shot at the intruder, who dived for cover and rolled behind the couch, returning fire. They continued the exchange as Chance backed into the hallway and through the bedroom. He slammed the door and lunged out the window.

With an *oomph* and a roll, Chance landed on a bed of pine needles. He got to his feet and glimpsed Destiny and Ayla before they disappeared into the forest. Chance sprinted toward them and didn't look back until he was secured behind a thicket.

The cabin sat silent.

Had Chance killed him? Or had the shooter escaped and was waiting for another opportunity?

Chance hurried to catch up with Ayla and Destiny. Which way had they gone? He surveyed the area and gave a low whistle. Two barks and Destiny came bounding through the forest.

He laughed as she jumped up, planting both front paws on his shoulders and covering his face with wet swipes of her tongue. "I missed you, too." Chance ruffled her tan and black fur, then took hold of her leash.

"I'm so glad you're okay." Ayla jogged to his side.

"We must keep moving. I'm not sure what happened to the shooter, but let's not assume he'll leave us alone. I need to notify my team." They continued walking and he called Commander Beckham Walsh.

"Where are you?"

Didn't the man ever start a conversation with hello?

"Sutler's working overtime to kill us." Chance provided an abbreviated explanation as they trudged through the terrain, ducking low-hanging branches and stepping over logs and downed trees.

"Do you have transportation?" Walsh asked.

"We're getting closer to where I hid my truck. I just hope it's still there."

"Get here as fast as you can. Make sure you're not followed." Did he sense irritation in Walsh's tone? "We'll meet at the Argo Hotel in Crofton. It's closed for sale, but I know the owners. Go through the northeast side door."

"Affirmative." Chance disconnected.

They reached a clearing, exposed without the cover of the trees. Chance increased his pace, and Ayla kept up. They tromped through the swaying wild grass, and the scents of pine and lilacs wafted on the light breeze.

Neither spoke until they crested the hill, where the blue

waters of Lewis and Clark Lake sparkled in the distance. The landmark provided Chance the navigation tool he needed to find his truck. With renewed fervor, he led them to the gravel road. "Keep close to the trees and bushes for cover."

"Got it."

The rough terrain made the quarter-mile hike seem longer than it was, but at the sight of his unmarked white pickup, Chance exhaled in relief. Even Destiny moved faster, straining against her leash. She, too, appreciated the find. Chance unlocked the doors, and the trio loaded inside.

Once he'd pulled onto the road, his gaze alternated between the rearview mirror and the road, searching for danger. "Keep an eye out for anything unusual."

Ayla shifted in the seat. "How does it work? Transferring me to another handler, I mean."

She was probably as eager to get away from him as he was to pass her over. They hadn't had a full conversation before encountering danger again. Proof he wasn't protector material. He was incapable of anything except finding fugitives. His specialty. The sooner he got her into Walsh's hands, the sooner he and Destiny would go after Myles Sutler and make him pay for what he'd done to Ezra Pullman.

"We're headed to meet them now."

"I'm sorry you're stuck babysitting me."

Chance winced. She'd overheard him. Great. "Listen, I didn't mean for it to come out that harshly. Destiny and I are skilled at hunting people. Until we arrest Sutler, you're not safe."

"Sure. I agree and understand." Except Ayla's tone and her turning away to face the window conveyed the complete opposite.

Nothing he said would sound right. He'd end up choking on his size-ten boot while simultaneously offending her. Better to remain silent.

Instead, he processed the earlier conversation with Ayla. Why hadn't Ezra gotten her out of the safe house sooner? And the bigger question—why hadn't he notified the team of the cabin location per protocol? "Let's go over the inter-actions you had with Ezra before the ambush."

"Why?" Ayla sighed, twisting to face him. "When the car came speeding to the house, I didn't think twice until Ezra said it wasn't him. Then I panicked." She glanced down, picking at her fingernails—obvious evasiveness that piqued Chance's suspicious nature. What was she hiding?

"What about the days before? Anything you tell me might help us find Sutler." He shifted the power to her, hoping she'd relent.

A long pause, then she said, "It was probably nothing." *Score.* "Try me."

"I overheard him talking on the phone. He mentioned 'the list' and told the person not to contact him unless they had information."

An informant? The rumored list, stolen from East-Side7's rival cartel, contained details on corrupt insiders within every part of the government and justice system. EastSide7 wanted that list to take their operations to the next level, and they'd do anything to get it. "You're cer-tain he said those words?"

Her green eyes narrowed to slits. "Yes, Sergeant Scru-tiny."

"Sorry, it comes with the gun-toting privileges," he quipped.

Her expression softened. "Touché."

They remained quiet for the rest of the drive into Crof-ton. At the sight of familiar Suburbans parked outside the old redbrick building, Chance's anxiety returned. Fancy lettering in the front window read Argo Hotel. Ayla exited before he'd shut off the engine. Chance quickly released

Destiny, opting to keep her off leash. She hopped down and gave a thorough shake of her tan and brown coat, then fell into step beside him.

Ayla was already walking up the steps to where Walsh waited on the porch. "I'm Commander Beckham Walsh." He shook her hand and held the door open, allowing her to enter first. He shot Chance a disapproving look and said, "Glad to see you made it without incident."

Chance swallowed the boulder of nervousness wedged in his throat, absorbing the verbal stab at his inability to protect Ayla. He didn't reply. Instead, averting his eyes, he trailed his boss into the building.

Decorative oriental rugs covered the wood floors, and antique furniture filled every conceivable space. Walsh led them into the sitting room where the rest of the task force waited. Destiny hurried to greet the other team K-9s in a flurry of tail wags and sniffs.

"Everyone, please introduce yourselves to Miss Du-Pree," Walsh said, walking to a chair farthest from the entry.

"FBI agent Tiandra Daugherty and K-9 Bosco."

"ATF agent Skyler Rios."

"DEA agent Graham Kenyon."

Each team member spoke, filling the space with their credentials, but Chance's pulse drummed in his ears, muting the conversation. He longed to impress them and prove he deserved to be there. The short eight months he'd been a part of the task force hadn't lessened his nervousness. Every interaction felt like a job interview.

"We represent most of the law enforcement alphabet, right, Chance?" Tiandra teased.

He blinked, entering the discussion. "Yes." His smile was so forced he worried his face would crack in half.

Ayla perched on a brown chair with cushioned arms.

The tension seemed to evaporate from her posture, and she smiled. "Thank you all for helping me."

Chance sat closest to her, quickly comprehending he'd chosen the most uncomfortable seat in the room.

"The owners vacated the premises, so speak freely," Walsh said. "We all loved Ezra and share in your grief."

Ayla averted her eyes, focusing instead on her folded hands in her lap.

"I'm sorry for your loss." DEA agent Graham Kenyon moved closer to her, taking Ayla's hands into his. His voice was tender, filled with compassion, and her demeanor softened. "Ezra spoke highly of you."

Though Graham had said nothing flirtatious, Ayla's response to him wove an unfamiliar feeling through Chance. Jealousy? No. He gritted his teeth and maintained a disinterested expression.

Deputy US Marshal Riker Kastell burst through the front door, his Dutch shepherd trotting off leash beside him. "Sorry I'm late," he said as he took a seat.

Walsh continued the meeting. "I've already briefed the team on the attempts on your lives," he explained, darting a glance at Chance.

He tried not to cringe under the man's scrutiny.

"Let's do a quick brief and get Chance and Ayla on their way to the new safe house," Walsh continued.

Chance blinked. Surely, he'd misunderstood.

"Cleanup continues at the old location," Graham said, "but the explosion destroyed everything."

"Probably what Myles and his gang intended," Riker inserted.

"I'll head to the state lab for the ballistics analysis from the mannequin," ATF agent Skyler Rios added.

"No offense, but what do you hope to gain from that?" Ayla asked.

"We'll document the bullets and casings recovered from both crime scenes, and when we find Sutler and his minions," Skyler said, "we'll confiscate their weapons and match them."

"More condemning evidence to convict them," Graham added.

"Conviction isn't the issue," Ayla said. "Keeping me alive is."

Chance's face warmed at the verbal slam to his incompetency.

Walsh's phone rang, and he stood. "I need to take this." He answered the call, exiting the room.

Chance rose and excused himself, following the commander into the dining area.

"Thanks, we'll get her transferred ASAP." Walsh disconnected and faced him. "That was the WitSec coordinator. Drive Miss DuPree to the safe house in Pender and stay there until further ordered."

"Sir, I need to speak with you." Chance glanced behind him, ensuring no one else had followed, then added, "Privately."

"Okay." Impatience wove through Walsh's expression.

"Ezra instructed Ayla to go to the cabin. He prepared to travel there before the ambush, and he didn't remove the antitheft device on the SUV." Chance paused. "Although that helped us find Ayla, both are failures to follow protocol."

Walsh frowned. "I can't disagree. And it's inconsistent with Ezra's character. He was a seasoned officer and knew better."

"Precisely."

"I'll notify the team." Walsh turned to leave.

"Sir, with all due respect—"

"I hate when people say that." Walsh sighed and faced

him, arms crossed. "It's a precursor to something I don't want to hear."

This was going well. "Destiny and I are at the top of our game. We have a one hundred percent success rate in finding fugitives. Locating Miss DuPree confirms that."

"Tavalla, you're on this team because I'm fully aware of your credentials," Walsh replied.

"Yes, sir, so I respectfully request another team member take over Miss DuPree's security. This allows Destiny and me to focus on hunting Sutler."

"Request considered." Walsh glanced at his phone.

Chance inhaled. Whew. He'd be done with Ayla.

"Request denied." Walsh returned his gaze to Chance. "Take Ayla to the safe house in Pender." He placed a hand on Chance's shoulder. "The team will centralize efforts on Sutler and keep you updated. Miss DuPree's safety is our top priority, along with finding the list."

"Affirmative," Chance said, forcing away the argument on his lips.

"And try not to die along the way."

Why wouldn't Walsh want to maximize Chance and Destiny's manhunt skills?

Chance gripped the steering wheel tighter, berating himself for not having a better counterargument and well-thought-out discussion points before he'd spoken to Walsh. He'd blown his one opportunity to convince the commander to reassign her protective detail. Aside from failing—which ultimately meant getting Ayla killed—he had no reasonable excuse to pass her off to another team member.

Why didn't Walsh understand the task force needed Chance and Destiny to find Sutler? *My ways are higher than your ways, and My thoughts than your thoughts.* The Scripture was like a slap upside his attitude. God obviously had other plans for his part in this mission. But hadn't God given him the ability to do his job? Didn't He want Chance and Destiny to maximize their skills?

"You're quiet," Ayla said, interrupting his mental diatribe.

"Processing information," he mumbled. Not a lie.

"We're headed to Pender? Where's that?"

"We're close."

"I assumed you'd leave me with someone else. Graham was so kind and spoke of Ezra like he'd known him forever," she said.

Exasperation wove through Chance. Of course, she'd name Graham. His natural ability to connect with others, especially women, was a skill Chance didn't possess. Though, truthfully, he'd deem his teammate's aptitude as nothing more than flirting. Except the thought of handing Ayla over to Graham ignited that strange jealousy in Chance again. No, it was only disappointment in not leading the manhunt. Jealousy required emotions for another person. That was not the case with Ayla. She was nothing more than his charge.

"All your team members are wonderful. Agent Skyler shared how NIBIN—that stands for the National Integrated Ballistics Identification Network," Ayla rambled on, as though Chance had never heard of the system, "contains ballistics evidence. She said the casings and bullets found at the scenes might connect to other EastSide7 crimes. Isn't that fascinating?"

"Uh-huh," Chance replied, barely listening.

"FBI agent Tiandra and K-9 Bosco are so in sync. You can see the strength of their relationship." Ayla's excitement increased as she persevered in voicing her elation about his team. "Who was the one that came in late with the beautiful Dutch shepherd?"

Chance gnawed on the question, reengaging himself

in the conversation. "Deputy US Marshal Riker Kastell and K-9 Ammo."

"That's right. I spaced on their names," Ayla said. "Bosco is a handsome guy, too. Tiandra said he was originally partnered with Skyler, but that recently changed. He's now partnered with Tiandra, allowing Skyler to train a new dog?"

"I guess," Chance mumbled.

"All the dogs are amazing."

In response to Ayla's comment, Destiny poked her head through the divider.

A smile burst through Chance's lips. "Yes, she meant you, too," he said, stroking her scruff. "She's an attention sponge."

Destiny licked his cheek, and he chuckled. Appreciation for his K-9 warmed Chance. She always knew how to cheer him up.

"How long have you two been together?"

"About four years. I couldn't have chosen a better partner."

"Is she the only female K-9 on the team?" Ayla started to reach for Destiny, then hesitated. "I should ask first."

"You can pet her. And yes, Destiny's the only female. Though that could change depending on whatever dog Skyler partners with."

Ayla allowed Destiny to smell her hand before touching her. "Aw, she's so soft." They rode in comfortable quiet for a few minutes before Ayla said, "I understand you're not thrilled with this arrangement. I wouldn't be either if I were you. I'm sorry you're stuck with me."

And now he felt like a jerk. He sighed. "It's not you."

"Suppose I believe that. What's your hesitation?"

That was the ultimate question. *When the team discovers I'm a fraud with only one skill—man hunting—they'll kick me off. I'm incapable of caring for or protecting a witness, or anyone else for that matter. Just as I failed Shel-*

ton when we were kids. The thought triggered Chance's defenses. Nope, he refused to look that ugly beast from his past in the face right now. Not yet.

"We're close," he replied dully, ignoring her question. "Keep your eyes out for a farmhouse."

He transitioned from Highway 35 to 15 and accelerated.

The landscape evolved from miles of cornfields, ready for harvest, to a cattle feedlot, wafting unpleasant scents into the truck.

Ayla groaned, covering her nose. "I'll never get used to that smell."

Chance snorted. "No one does. Maybe your senses grow dull to it or something."

"No kidding."

They rounded a hill, and based upon Chance's cell phone GPS directions, they were nearing the Pender town limits. The safe house sat on the west edge of an abandoned farm. He exited the county highway and turned onto an unpaved road.

Rocks and gravel pinged the underside of his truck. Deep grooves in the road worn by extended neglect and overuse had Chance battling to stay centered. In his peripheral vision, a black pickup kicked up dust and headed toward them on a dirt path on the right.

His instincts flared, and the hairs on his neck rose. With one eye on the road and the other on the oncoming vehicle, he mentally worked through his options. He jerked the wheel, taking an unexpected turn at the next intersection. Harvest season was near, and the corn was tall and dry. Chance hoped it provided them cover as he searched for another exit.

"I'm guessing you've already noticed them," Ayla said.

"Yeah." Chance flicked a glance at her. "Stay low in the seat, but don't take off your seat belt."

"Negative."

That got his attention, and he jerked to look at her. "What?"

Ayla held the pistol from the cabin.

"What are you doing?"

The truck behind them turned but kept a distance. Tinted windows combined with the sun's glare made identifying the driver and passenger impossible. From the little he could make out, both wore sunglasses and hoodies. The wrong attire for the balmy autumn air.

"We're driving away from the safe house," Ayla said.

"Yes, I'm aware of that." The last thing he needed was her nitpicking his every move.

"You agree we're in danger?"

Before Chance replied, Ayla reached for his cell phone and called 9-1-1, reporting the vehicle.

"Don't shoot yet," Chance warned. "It could be a hot rod trying to pass us." The years of public scrutiny over law enforcement prompted his hesitation. A premature reaction could result in a bad outcome.

"Yeah, right." Ayla's tone was thick with sarcasm as she positioned in the seat.

"Destiny, down!"

The dog quickly disappeared into her kennel, and Chance slid the divider closed.

Ayla rolled down her window.

"What're you doing?" Her take-charge personality threw Chance, but he had no time to process the information before the massive push bar on the truck's grille roared into his rearview mirror.

A slam from behind thrust them forward, and the vehicle fishtailed.

Chance gripped the steering wheel tighter, fighting the force trying to veer them off into the ditch.

FOUR

The hit sent Ayla off balance, and she smacked her arm on the window frame, nearly knocking the gun from her hand. Destiny yelped from her kennel, causing righteous indignation to override her fear.

"It's okay, girl." Chance's tone was calm, but Ayla heard the underlying fury. "Can you get a clean shot?"

"Definitely." She repositioned and aimed.

One trigger squeeze sent the hoodlums' vehicle swerving.

"Excellent!" Chance maneuvered the truck to the side, avoiding another blow. "How does EastSide7 keep finding us?"

The question was rhetorical, and Ayla didn't respond. She didn't need to.

She shot again, this time striking the windshield with two consecutive rounds. Though she'd hit her mark, the pursuers remained dangerously close.

Gunshots pelted their truck, shattering Ayla's side mirror. She ducked inside, then leaned out again and returned fire. "They're relentless."

"You're doing great," Chance commended.

The shooters' engine revved, and another collision sent them swerving dangerously close to a steep ditch. Chance recovered, centering the vehicle on the road.

Ayla scanned for a possible detour. The road drew out

in a long stretch, spanning the horizon. If he drove into the ditch, they'd most likely get stuck, tear off a tire, roll the truck or ruin the drive train. And the EastSide7 shooters would kill them. Not an option.

Several more rounds pelted Chance's vehicle.

"I've had enough of these guys."

Ayla peeked out and returned fire, ducking inside just as Chance's side mirror shattered. "There!" She gestured ahead.

A grove lined with mature oaks on one edge and a narrow sandy shoulder on the other provided a onetime opportunity to lose the shooters. There was no room for mistakes.

"Hang on." Chance accelerated.

Ayla closed her window and slid down in her seat.

The roar of the pursuers' vehicle confirmed they remained close, but Ayla didn't dare turn around to see.

"Come on." Chance's tone was low, menacing. "Line up with me."

Ayla braced for another hit, eyes pinned on Chance. He yanked the wheel, and the pursuing truck blazed past them, straight into the grove.

Metal collided with wood in a sickening slam that reverberated through the country landscape. Ayla looked out the window, spotting the pickup's front end embedded in a tree trunk.

Smoke fumed from the hood.

"Well done!" She settled into her seat. "That was too cool!"

Chance grinned, lifting a palm for a one-handed high five. "That'll keep them off our tail for a little while."

"Wow! Great driving." Ayla didn't hide her admiration.

"Thanks to your exceptional shooting." He made a U-turn and sped in the opposite direction, taking a left at the next intersection. When he'd driven a reasonable distance from the shooters, he pulled to the side of the road behind an abandoned Morton building and disconnected his seat belt. He tugged the divider open and checked on Destiny.

Ayla twisted around to see, but Chance blocked the narrow space. "Is she all right?"

"Yeah, she's okay." He sat back down and Destiny's furry muzzle appeared between them.

"Hey, pretty girl, you did great," Ayla soothed.

Chance cooed, stroking the dog's dark fur. "You're okay. It's all over now." She responded with a muffled bark.

Ayla grinned. "I've never heard a dog make that sound."

"I call it her *mrff*," Chance explained, offering one last scratch under her scruff. "Let's get out of here."

"Are you sure she's okay?"

"Yep, the topper and equipment in the bed might be a different story, but no bullets penetrated the kennel, from what I can see. She's secure in there." Chance snapped his seat belt before shifting into gear and pulling away. "Destiny is tough, albeit a little shook up at the moment."

"Now what?"

"New plan." Chance used his hands-free device and called Walsh on speakerphone.

"What's up?" the commander answered in greeting.

"We had visitors at Pender." Chance added, "Oh, and we need responding units to a tree versus pickup at mile marker twenty-five on County Road 192." He offered a quick synopsis of what had happened.

"Unbelievable!" Walsh boomed through the line.

"How did they find us?" Chance asked.

Walsh remained silent, and they heard tapping sounds in the background.

"We have a le—"

"Don't say it," Walsh said. "Toss this phone as soon as we hang up. Call me from the burner."

"Roger that." Chance disconnected and stopped in the middle of the road. He got out, placed his cell phone under the front tire, hopped into the truck and pulled forward. Satisfied by the crunch, he accelerated. "In the glovebox is a phone."

"You keep burner cells on hand?" Ayla asked.

"Yes, for occasions like this."

"Doesn't Commander Walsh start conversations with hello?"

Chance chuckled. "Noticed that, too?"

"Yeah."

"Please call the only number saved and put it on speakerphone."

Ayla withdrew the device and did as Chance requested.

The line rang once before Walsh answered, "Okay, I'm texting an address to you."

Ayla grinned in response to Walsh's lack of greeting.

"This is the horse ranch I share with my sister, Marissa. I'll let her know to expect you."

An expression Ayla couldn't define crossed Chance's face. "With all due respect—" He paused, then said, "Sir, will she require protection detail as well?"

Walsh's chortle bounced through the line. "A decade in the marines provided her with those skills. She can handle her own."

Chance blushed, and Ayla tamped down her grin. What was that about?

"Roger that."

They disconnected and the screen came to life with a picture of a map. "It's near Ponca State Park."

"Okay," Chance said. "Just in case, we're taking the long way there."

"This is unreal." She sighed. "There's no doubt in my

mind your system has a leak." Ayla expected Chance to go off, defending his own.

Instead, he replied, "No argument here, and Walsh's order to go to his personal property tells me he agrees. Your shooting skills are impressive. I hope this doesn't offend you, but I viewed you as a damsel in distress. You're not even close to that."

"That's an unexpected compliment, though I admit, firearm skills weren't my first choice. Ezra insisted I have the training necessary to defend myself since he was unable to stay with me 24-7." Ayla shrugged. "He said I had to be prepared to fight. We spent countless hours training. I'm grateful for that, though." She didn't want to believe Ezra was compromised, but the ambush at the safe house left her suspicious and questioning everything and everyone.

"He was an amazing man." Chance fixated a little too hard on the windshield. "Ezra trained me, too."

She blinked. "Really?"

"Don't sound so surprised."

"I didn't mean it that way." How did she mean it?

"He was my instructor when I first joined the marshals."

Ayla sucked in a breath, wondering how much to share. "I trusted him." She shifted away from him, not wanting to confess she might've assumed incorrectly about Ezra. Still, he'd told her to leave the house, certain she was in danger. Or had he changed his mind and felt bad about selling her out to Sutler's men?

"I can't imagine what you've been through." The kindness in Chance's tone nearly undid her.

Unwilling for him to see her quivering lip threatening to betray her resolve, she turned to look out the window. "Do you ever dream of getting a do-over in life?"

"All the time."

Something unspoken in his response piqued Ayla's curiosity, but she didn't press. "Me, too. I never should've gone there."

"Where?"

She glanced at him. Confusion clouded Chance's handsome features. Hadn't he read her file? "To Judge Warden's house."

"We have a long drive if you want to talk about it." His burner phone rang, interrupting the conversation. "Please answer and put it on speaker."

Grateful for the interruption and the chance to pull herself together, Ayla did as he asked.

"Ayla," Walsh said in greeting.

"I'm here," she answered, shooting a he-did-it-again glance at Chance. He gave a quick nod.

"The team has discovered evidence of conversations between Ezra and an unidentified person," Walsh said.

Concern wove through her. "Was it bad?" The question concealed what she really meant. *Was Ezra bad?*

"There are a few questionable messages that we're hoping you can help us decipher." She recognized Graham's voice.

"I'll try."

"Twice in the texts we see the phrase, 'you'll know George,'" Graham said. "Does that mean anything to you?"

"That's the name I gave the ballistics mannequin Ezra and I trained with," Ayla said, but the words lingered in her mind with a twinge of familiarity.

The line went quiet for several seconds. "All right. We'll keep digging through the messages," Walsh said. "Advise when you get to the next location."

"Affirmative," Chance said before Ayla disconnected.

"That is so strange. Why mention George?" Ayla asked.

"Was anyone else aware of the nickname?"

"No." Ayla tapped a finger against her lips. "I hate this.

I don't want to believe Ezra was working for EastSide7, but the list is proof more than one person in the judicial system has fallen prey to their deceptive ways."

"Have you ever seen it? The list?"

"No, I've just heard the rumors."

"I knew Ezra a long time, and I cannot wrap my mind around him being dirty, but, like you said, it's not inconceivable." Chance flipped on the air conditioner, filling the cab with a cool wave and a soft hum. "Earlier you talked about a do-over. Can you tell me more?"

Why had she opened her big mouth? Ayla sighed. "I doubt it will help anything."

"We have a long drive. Consider it conversation." He shot her what she surmised was his attempt at an encouraging smile.

She feared she'd melt under his knockout gaze. Chance had an alluring quality along with his good looks. But his eyes revealed the hard truth. He needed to work the case, and she was an information channel. Nothing more. She'd need to remember that.

Would it hurt to tell him? Everything was in the file. The idea of repeating the story again made her nauseous. Each time she spoke of it dragged her into the moment, made her relive the terror. "I never should've gone there." She repeated the self-loathing mantra she'd recited a hundred times.

Ayla sank in the seat, her mind replaying the past six months in excruciating detail. The strenuous training, hiding from danger and learning to defend herself were useless if Chance and his team didn't find the list and arrest Myles Sutler soon. He and the EastSide7 gang wouldn't stop until they'd killed Ayla.

Ezra had taught her a lot, and she'd forever be grateful, but she had no hope of fighting off an entire gang without serious help. She'd spent too much time alone, talking to a mannequin and praying without ceasing. Now she had the opportunity to discuss her predicament with someone who'd understand. Why was she hesitating?

She scanned Chance again. *Just do it.* "I worked late that Friday night in the office to catch up before the weekend."

"Was that normal?"

"Yes. I have nothing but my career." Ayla bit her lip. Why had she confessed her pathetic personal life to him?

Destiny poked her head through the divider, touching her cold nose to Ayla's cheek, then settled where she could look at Ayla. The dog's facial coloring gave the impression of eyebrows. She lifted one as if to say, *I understand.* Ayla grinned and stroked the shepherd.

"Destiny and I totally get living the job," Chance said.

"I suppose you do."

"K-9 teams are required to train daily to maintain our skills." Chance gave a one-shoulder shrug. "Unless we're dodging killers."

"You never take breaks?" Ayla gaped at him. Her long work hours were self-imposed. She couldn't imagine such a rigorous schedule. Chance's dedication impressed her.

"We can't. Destiny thinks it's fun, so I try to focus on that mind-set, too."

The dog panted softly, as if in agreement.

"Anyway, sorry to interrupt," Chance said. "Please continue."

"I had prepared to leave the office when I realized during an earlier meeting with RJ—er, Judge Warden," she corrected herself, not wanting to use his first name, "we'd accidentally swapped phones and neither of us had the luxury of going an entire weekend without them. Although knowing what I do now, I'd gladly have waited."

"What happened next?" Chance prodded.

"I tried calling, but he didn't answer my cell phone or his landline. I figured if he'd discovered the mix-up, he might not feel comfortable answering mine."

"But why not pick up his landline?"

"Ignoring that wasn't unusual. He had voice mail set up on it and often screened calls. I waited an hour after leaving messages, and when he didn't respond, I drove to his house." Ayla shifted in the seat, tucking one leg under her thigh. "I didn't realize how late it was until I was on my way and figured if there were lights on, I'd knock, and if not, I'd try again in the morning."

"None of that seems unreasonable."

Ayla released an unladylike snort. "My whole life is a disaster because I couldn't bear to be without a cell phone."

"They're standard equipment for everyone these days. Your actions were reasonable," Chance said. "What happened when you got to Warden's?"

She appreciated his remarks. She'd spent too much time beating herself up, and it was easy to get stuck in that loop. "There were lights on in his study, but the rest of the house was dark, so I assumed Octavia, his wife, was asleep. I walked around to the backyard to enter through the kitchen door."

"The judge didn't mind you walking in?"

Ayla shook her head. "Our families are close. I practically grew up there after my father passed away."

A flash of something indescribable passed through Chance's eyes. He worked his jaw but didn't comment.

"When I got to the rear porch, I heard loud voices. Not just arguing, out-of-control fighting." Ayla glanced out the window, knowing the situation made her look nosy. "I peeked inside and saw Myles Sutler with RJ."

"You knew Sutler?"

"Not at the time. I sort of recognized him, but not really. I know that makes no sense."

"No, I get it."

"It happens a lot to me after handling the number of files and cases I do. They all blend and I'm never sure if I recognize someone or if I've read their criminal case a hundred times." At first, she'd feared talking, but now she rambled. Maybe Chance hadn't noticed.

"Go on." He either didn't mind or he was politely telling her to get to the point.

"They were fighting about 'the list.' In that moment, I wasn't aware of what that meant, and honestly didn't care. But I was sort of stuck standing there since they'd realize I'd eavesdropped if I came out of hiding. They calmed down and talked to each other easily, and I wondered if I'd been wrong about the other guy. Maybe it wasn't Myles. Just another cop wanting a warrant. RJ got irritated with cops coming over after hours." Ayla paused. "Octavia, too. She's no fan of law enforcement, mainly for that reason."

"Was she there?" Chance asked.

"I didn't find out until later that she wasn't home, which turned out to be a good thing. I hate to think what Myles would've done..." Her voice trailed off. "Anyway, I'd decided to wait because I needed my phone. But then Myles became infuriated, demanding RJ hand it over." Ayla didn't share how watching the fight had frozen her in place, the way dissension always did. Pulling her under crushing waves of anxiety.

Chance's question interrupted her thoughts. "How did the judge respond?"

The remainder of the scene played out in front of Ayla on an endless reel. "He adamantly refused."

"But he claimed to have the list?" Chance asked.

"I never heard him confess that. Myles tried bribing him. That infuriated RJ and confused me. It wasn't inconceivable he was a cop trying to bribe RJ for a warrant, but it wasn't the norm."

"You'd seen Judge Warden accept bribes?"

The question immobilized Ayla with an impossible ultimatum. Thoughts of her father's deception barreled into her. If she didn't answer truthfully, Chance would pick up on it. If she answered honestly, she'd paint RJ as a criminal. "I never witnessed him doing it." Technically, that was true.

"And you had no clue who Sutler was during all this time?"

"Nope." Did she hear accusation or disbelief in his tone? Ayla studied him, but his demeanor remained calm. He was a cop—perhaps his questions were inquisitive, investigative. "I turned to leave just as Myles stabbed RJ. I freaked out. I spun on my heel, desperate to escape before he saw me, but I tripped over a planter on the porch. I'd practically rung a gong, drawing attention to myself. Can you believe that? And in slow motion, Myles and I exchanged a quick look, while RJ yelled for me to run away. Myles chased me, but I hid in the neighbor's garage. After he left, I checked on RJ." She paused, swallowing the lump in her throat. "He was dead. Then I drove straight to the police department."

"That was smart."

"After I reported the incident and specified the strange tattoo I'd seen on Myles's neck, it was like someone hit an alarm. Suddenly I'm tossed to Deputy US Marshal Ezra Pullman and thrown into WitSec because I've identified RJ's killer as the leader of EastSide7."

"Then the cops arrest Sutler, putting you on his kill list, because as the only witness to the murder, he has to eliminate you before the trial," Chance concluded.

"Exactly. Then it went from bad to worse when Myles escaped during his prison transport." And Ayla's nightmare continued.

Chance considered details that didn't resonate well with him. Too many factors pointed to an insider working on behalf of EastSide7. Had Ezra sent Ayla to the cabin intending to kill her there? If so, why warn her beforehand if he planned to hand her over to the gang and wash his hands of the act itself? But if he feared the house was compromised, why hadn't he notified the task force and followed protocol? Nothing in the case made sense. Worse, Sutler and EastSide7 stayed a step ahead.

He turned off the main highway onto a private road. Though paved, the narrow path permitted one vehicle at a time. The rolling hill landscape further complicated Chance's cautious approach. Thick trees canopied overhead, providing shade from the afternoon sun that peeked through the leaves at intervals.

Ayla moved forward in her seat, gaping out the windshield. "This is incredible."

"Yeah, I'd definitely live here," Chance replied, mesmerized by the picturesque scene unfolding before him. Compared to the small apartment he shared with Destiny, the freedom of living in the country had him reconsidering his housing options.

Where had Ayla lived prior to being thrust into witness protection? Curiosity had him contemplating questions to gather the information without being nosey. No. That was none of his business and completely irrelevant to the case. He reminded himself to maintain an emotional distance, but the time they spent together ignited his curiosity and made him want to know her better.

"Is that the place?" Ayla pointed at a split rail fence that sprawled across the landscape, dividing square sections within the property.

Chance glanced at the map. "Yeah, if the address is correct."

He turned off the paved road onto a gray gravel path that wove through a copse of behemoth cottonwood trees. Lush green grass carpeted the land on both sides. Chance approached an open gate between the split rail fence, and he entered, keeping his speed to a crawl.

He pulled through an archway suspended by supporting log posts and a maple sign that read Meadowlark Lane Ranch in black wrought iron letters. The gravel road curved into a grove of bordering trees, and the house sat a half mile from the main entrance, hidden by the foliage.

"Wow," Ayla whispered.

"Yeah. Exactly." Chance slowed, allowing her to absorb the beautiful atmosphere. Even Destiny had popped her head through the divider, joining them in their quiet reverie.

He pulled up to the ranch-style house constructed of gray siding and trimmed in white. An inviting wraparound porch overshadowed the barn doors and stone exterior leading to a walkout basement. Nestled between massive oak and maple trees, corrals stretched out on the well-kept grounds, where a variety of horses meandered within the fenced borders.

Chance parked, shutting off the engine. "Walsh said Marissa would expect us."

"If this is my new safe house, I'm okay with it," Ayla breathed.

He grinned. "Not what I pictured when he said 'horse ranch.'"

"Right?" She released her seat belt and slid out of the vehicle.

Ayla met him at the front of the truck just as a petite

woman stepped out the door and paused on the porch. "Chance and Ayla, welcome to Meadowlark Lane Ranch."

She descended the stone stairs and approached with a smile, her auburn ponytail bouncing with each step. Chance guessed she stood about five feet two inches, and she wore jeans and boots with a flat heel. Rolled-up sleeves of her teal cotton shirt revealed a smart watch on her right wrist, indicating she was left-handed. He'd guess her to be in her midthirties, maybe forty. Chance knew better than to ask a woman her age. She oozed confidence, but not arrogance, and kindness emanated from her striking blue eyes. Though her attire was modest, her build testified to regular workouts. Something about Marissa Walsh, ex-marine, said, "Don't mess with me." An orange tabby trailed her like a dog, staying close to her side.

"Thanks for having us." Ayla extended a hand, which Marissa returned with a shake.

"Sorry to invade your home." Chance turned and released Destiny.

"Chance, should you wait?" Ayla moved to his side. "Will she be okay with a cat?"

He glanced down, never having considered the question, since he wasn't around cats normally. "Guess we'll find out."

The tabby strolled to the shepherd, and they offered each other a customary disinterested sniffing before the feline returned to sit beside Marissa.

"Zink beat me to the greeting," she snickered. "I'm Marissa Walsh," she said to Ayla and Chance while extending her hand to Destiny. The dog sniffed and wagged her tail, approving the petting to come. Marissa smiled and stroked Destiny's head. "Hello, beautiful."

"Duly noted, Destiny approves of cats," Chance replied.

"Zink's clueless he's a cat. He struts around thinking

he's a human and irresistible to everyone. Too bad we don't all live with that kind of confidence and assurance." Marissa chortled. "Though I can name a few guys in my unit who did."

"I wouldn't mind being irresistible," Chance joked, looking at Ayla. His neck warmed. Why had he said that?

She responded with a quizzical tilt of her head, and he pretended not to notice.

"No bags?" Marissa quirked an auburn brow.

"Just mine." Chance withdrew his duffel bag from the back seat, the realization slamming into him.

Ayla had no belongings. Why hadn't he offered to take her shopping? He winced. Once more, he'd failed to take care of his charge. "Ayla, let's run back to town and grab some things for you."

She blinked. "In all the chaos, I forgot all about it."

Guilt assuaged Chance again.

"No worries. Without breaking protocol— something my brother wouldn't do—Becky provided a mini rundown of your situation and said you'd need civvies," Marissa replied.

Ayla blinked at the unfamiliar name.

"Civilian attire," Chance interpreted, then mouthed *Becky?* "I wasn't aware Commander Walsh was married. Not that I needed to be. We don't discuss personal stuff at work." Good grief, he was rambling.

Marissa glanced over her shoulder. "He's not. Becky is his family nickname." She winked.

Ayla giggled, and Chance had to force himself not to laugh aloud. "Roger that."

Marissa grinned. "Sorry, old habits die hard. I've called Beckham that since we were kids." She leaned in and lowered her voice. "He hates it, which is why I continue to do it."

They laughed.

"I've got supplies for you. Don't worry, Ayla, clothes aren't a problem. You're about the same size as me, and Becky insists we keep extra clothing here."

"Thank you," Ayla said. "Ezra had taught me to have no attachments to belongings because the time might come when we'd have to…" She hesitated, as if choosing her words carefully. "Relocate without notice," she finally added. "So I learned to travel light."

Zink strolled to her, and Ayla knelt, extending a hand and stroking his orange fur.

"He loves being held," Marissa said.

Ayla lifted Zink, and he folded into her arms, emitting a soft purr.

Chance surveyed her, concluding there were cat people and dog people. Destiny nudged his hand. He would forever be a dog person. "Want to check out the place?"

Without waiting for him, Destiny led the way down the lane toward the horse standing near the fence.

"She's got the right idea. Come on and I'll show you around." Marissa strode past them, and they fell into line behind her.

"I dare you to call Commander Walsh *Becky* when you talk to him next," Ayla whispered to Chance.

"I like my career. Nothing doing."

Destiny had busied herself sniffing the area near a massive horse's hooves while maintaining a healthy distance. "Destiny," Chance called. The shepherd looked up and trotted to his side.

"Are you familiar with horses?" Marissa walked to the largest horse Chance had ever seen. The beautiful black animal stood beside the fence and gave a soft snort at her approach.

"No, just an admirer," Chance replied.

"I've ridden a few times, but that's it," Ayla said.

"There's nothing like them. They're intuitive, sensing your mood. Personally, I believe they read our body language, interpreting our thoughts, even before we do." Marissa leaned with her back to the animal, and he hovered, placing his head on her shoulder. "This is Shadow. We call him Shad for short. He's a Percheron we rescued." She stroked his strong muzzle. "Later, I'll show you where their treats are. He's very food motivated. Feed Shad an apple and he's forever devoted."

He whinnied, bobbing his head, and Ayla laughed. "Is that confirmation?"

"Absolutely. You'll need to know the grounds, so let me show you around here, then we'll head inside. Chance, you might want to pull your truck into the Morton building behind the barn."

"Roger that." Chance glanced where Marissa gestured at the considerable structure and comprehended her meaning. They needed to stay off the radar as much as possible.

"This place is amazing." Wistfulness hung in Ayla's voice.

"Yes. It didn't start out that way. Becky and I worked hard to restore it. He did a lot when I was overseas. I was grateful to return here." Marissa led them along the stone path toward a bulky building painted to match the house.

Chance studied the woman. "Commander Walsh mentioned you were in the marines."

Marissa paused and faced him, a hardness returning to her expression. "Yep, two tours in the sandbox."

Ayla blinked. "What?"

"The Middle East," Marissa clarified. "Not the answer you expected?" She tilted her head in a sassy challenge.

He'd thought she'd stayed at a US base, not seen real war action. "No. I— You—" Good gravy, he was stuttering.

"That was a long time ago. This is my life now." Marissa headed for the barn. "Let me show you the property, and we'll come back out here afterward."

They followed her to the unassuming barn, but when she opened the doors, they gaped at the interior. They entered, perusing the space.

The pristine stone floor held not a trace of dirt, and ten gated stalls, five on each side, were fixed with dark wood and iron gates, complete with latches and engraved nameplates beneath each stall. The scents of hay and horses lingered in the air, sweet and inviting yet a little off-putting.

"I used to hate the smell," Marissa said. "But now it's comforting."

Chance marveled at how she picked up on his reaction even without words.

"We'll muck the stalls before we corral the horses." Marissa's voice echoed in the room.

He mouthed *we?* to Ayla, and she shrugged and said, "Gotta earn our keep."

"How many horses do you have?" he asked.

"Twenty acres of land and eight rescues."

Chance inwardly winced, calculating the amount of mucking that required. "Beck, er, Commander Walsh owns all of this?" he asked, not attempting to hide his surprise.

Ayla turned in a slow circle, then shot him a grin.

"We both do," Marissa replied. "It's our combined retirement investment, since we're loners." A sadness passed in her eyes, but she quickly blinked it away, a smile replacing the expression that Chance wondered if he'd imagined.

"Shelton and I can't agree enough to share a candy bar. I can't imagine an entire ranch," Chance replied, catching a curious glance from Ayla.

"Shelton?"

"My little brother."

"You have siblings?" She gave a slight nod, probing him to elaborate.

He didn't. Instead, he redirected. "You rescue, not breed?"

"Yes, let's go out and I'll introduce you to the family." Marissa led them from the barn and onto the path.

Chance quickly assessed she moved fast, so they had to keep up or get left behind. They strolled along the split rail fence, and she pointed to where two horses grazed near Shadow.

"The white one, Lady, is an Arabian." She gestured to a second horse, light gray with small white splotches. "That's Tinkerbell, a dapple gray. We adopted them together from a kill pen because the previous owners had abandoned them."

Ayla gasped. "That's horrible."

"All of them have sad stories. Too often, that's the case with rescues. They're living proof God provides second chances." Marissa moved farther along the fence and paused where three horses grazed a few feet beyond her. "Arrow is the buckskin." She pointed to a brown horse with a black tail. "Those two are quarter horses. The chestnut paint with white blocks is Caesar, and the other is Czar. He thinks he runs the place."

Ayla and Chance strode beside one another, her hand occasionally brushing his. He fought the urge not to reach for her. They persisted along the path where two horses stood beneath cottonwood trees.

Marissa climbed onto the fence and sat, her legs dangling. "Those two are our laziest rescues. Royal is the larger one. He's a thoroughbred, sent to the kill pen because the owners figured he'd served his purpose after he'd earned them thousands of dollars. Now he's happy to just meander. The Appaloosa," she said as she gestured toward a black horse with a white rear splotched with black spots, "is Dixie." Marissa whistled, and the animals lifted their heads and trotted to meet her at the fence.

"You call them like dogs?" Ayla asked, voicing Chance's unspoken question.

"Yep, they're just giant puppies."

Destiny gave a *harrumph*, eliciting laughter.

"No offense," Marissa said, stroking the dog's head.

The horses gazed curiously at them, and Chance shifted closer, touching Dixie's velvety nose.

Marissa turned to face them, her blue eyes darkened as though clouds passed over the irises. "Her story is the worst, and not one I talk about. Makes me angry. But suffice it to say, she's loved now."

The white Arabian closed in, hanging her head over the fence.

"Lady has major issues with FOMO," Marissa explained.

"What's that?" Chance asked, thoroughly confused.

"Fear of missing out," Ayla interpreted.

He chuckled and reached over, touching Lady's neck. "There are little knots in her mane."

"They're called fairy knots, since folklore says fairies come out at night to ride the special horses. They tie knots in the horse's mane to hang on," Marissa explained.

"How fun," Ayla said, grinning. "You should write a children's book about that."

"Did you name them?" Chance asked, still stroking Lady's neck.

"Nope, that's what they came with. It's against the unspoken horse ownership rules to change a horse's name." She hopped down and brushed off her hands. "Well, how about if we walk back? Are you two hungry?"

"Yes," Ayla blurted.

"I like you." Marissa laughed. "Gotta appreciate a sister in Christ who knows what she wants."

"Sorry, it's been a long day." A blush covered Ayla's cheeks.

Food. How had Chance not thought to feed her? He really was failing at this job.

"How did you know I was a Christian?" Ayla asked.

"His love is written all over your face," Marissa replied.

Chance studied Ayla. She radiated beauty for sure.

"Come on up to the house and I'll fix lunch." Without waiting for a reply, Marissa spun on her heel.

"Coming?" Ayla asked, jerking him out of his reverie.

"Yeah. Right behind you." He paused, not wanting to leave, and stroked Royal's soft muzzle. Long eyelashes shadowed the animal's dark eyes, and he exuded peace.

He glanced out at the expansive property, wondering when was the last time he'd experienced peace.

"Chance?" Ayla called.

He jogged in her direction, Destiny beside him. At least he didn't need to worry about them being traced here. And after all they'd endured, a little rest and relaxation sounded fabulous.

FIVE

If the property hadn't been mind-blowing enough, the house finished the job. Ayla stood amazed at the gorgeous open-concept home. An enormous stone fireplace centered the living space, with the kitchen and dining area opposite the living room.

Marissa led them down the hallway with two bedrooms on each side. "Ayla, take this one."

She pushed open the door, and Ayla gasped at the massive four-poster bed and the tall windows that filled the space with light. "Thank you." The comment seemed inadequate considering the accommodations.

"Chance, you and Destiny take the room across the hall."

Curious, Ayla peered around him to the similarly decorated bedroom. Marissa moved to the large accordion closet doors and tugged them open. She withdrew a dog cot and placed it near the bed. "For you, Destiny."

The shepherd trotted to it and climbed on with a sigh. She nestled down and closed her eyes.

"She approves." Chance chuckled.

"This house is incredible," Ayla said.

Marissa shrugged. "Becky and I enjoy working on it. We call the place a labor of love. My room is next to yours, and the last bedroom is Becky's. Go ahead and look around while I pull together lunch for us."

"You don't have to tell me twice," Ayla said.

Marissa smiled. "There are clothes in your bedroom closet. Help yourself to whatever you like. Nothing fancy, but they're clean." With that, she left Ayla and Chance.

"Up for a little exploring?"

"Definitely," Chance replied. "All righty, let's see what Becky built."

Ayla giggled, and they moved through the house. A set of stairs near the living room led to the basement, though it was unlike any Ayla had ever seen.

A large pool table stood to one side, and to the other, a massive screen in front of a sectional couch. "It's like a personal movie theater."

Chance strode to the sofa. "Every seat is a recliner. I need Commander Walsh to be my best friend."

Ayla gestured wide. "But wait, there's more."

Chance hopped to his feet, and they completed the tour. The basement held another bedroom and bathroom, and large windows allowed copious amounts of light, making the space bright and inviting.

Marissa met them at the steps, a cell phone pressed against her cheek. "Hold on, Becky, here's Chance." She passed him the phone, then ran up the stairs.

He took it and placed it on speakerphone. "Ayla is here with me."

"Call me Becky and I'll hurt you."

Ayla smothered a chuckle, and Chance grinned. "Roger that."

"Marissa will provide Ayla a cheap phone we keep at the house. The team is still working on the messages between Ezra and the unknown party."

"The phrase 'you'll know George' is stuck in my

brain," Ayla said. "I can't recall where I've heard it, but it's strangely familiar."

"If you come up with anything, notify me immediately."

"I will," Ayla assured him.

"One thing we've found is the mention of the list several times."

Chance met Ayla's eyes. "In what context?" he asked.

"The unknown party implies possession of it."

"Is it possible Judge Warden hid or held on to it as a bribe to get more money?" Chance asked.

Ayla bristled. "Don't jump to assumptions."

"I'm just talking through the idea." He quirked a brow.

Had Ayla spoken too soon? Why did she always jump in when she should remain silent? "Is Ezra's part of the conversation incriminating?"

"I can't answer that just yet, but Ayla's right," Beckham said.

Her muscles relaxed slightly.

"We must consider all the options," Beckham continued. "If Ezra tried working some kind of deal, we'll find the evidence. Advise if you come up with anything helpful."

"Will do." Chance disconnected.

"Has anyone checked on Octavia?" Ayla asked him.

Chance shook his head. "They questioned her initially and cleared her since she was out of town at the time of the murder."

"Not as a suspect. I meant check on her to see if she's in danger."

"Why?"

"Only two places come to mind where RJ might've hidden the list—the office, which seems unlikely, or his house."

"I'll call Walsh while I grab Destiny's supplies from the

truck. I need to move it into the Morton building." Chance headed for the door.

Ayla returned to the bedroom and looked through the clothing assortment. Marissa was right—they wore the same size, and the options were appealing. She maneuvered around the living area, glancing at the pictures placed on the mantel and side tables. One of Marissa in fatigues caught her eye, and she picked it up. In the photo, Marissa stood in front a large piece of equipment, similar to a Humvee, holding a rifle. A second photo of Commander Walsh grinning wide atop a palomino horse and wearing a black Stetson also intrigued her. Somehow it reminded Ayla of his humanness and the kindness he'd extended in offering his personal home for her stay.

Lord, please don't let Myles and his men find me here.

A plaque on the wall read, As for me and my house, we will serve the Lord. She hadn't realized Walsh was a man of faith, and the knowledge brought her a tremendous sense of peace.

Chance returned carrying a bag. "Wait until you see the Morton building. There's a huge pickup and horse trailer inside."

"Somehow, that doesn't surprise me."

"Lunch is served," Marissa called.

They walked to the kitchen and sat at the massive wood table with platters of cheese, meat, fruit and vegetables, enough for a crowd.

"Would you mind if I set up an area for Destiny to eat?" Chance asked, lifting the bag.

"Not at all." Marissa turned and set a mat on the floor, adding two large orange porcelain bowls.

Chance filled the bowls with water and kibble. "There ya go, girl. Enjoy." Destiny walked to his side and sniffed the offerings before lapping at the water.

Chance and Ayla washed their hands at the sink, then took their seats at the table. Marissa offered a prayer of thanks then passed Ayla a cheap cell phone. "It's all charged and ready to go. Becky will contact you directly on it."

Ayla pocketed the device. "Thank you."

Chance had no qualms about loading his plate with a double-decker club sandwich, fruit and chips. She glanced at Marissa, who winked. In contrast, Ayla had several slices of meat and cheese, fruits, and vegetables.

He glanced at their plates. "Have something against bread?" he asked before taking a bite of his sandwich.

Ayla glared at him. "No, it has something against me." She hated talking about her dietary restrictions. People tended to either offer unwanted medical advice or act like she was ridiculous.

"I understand that," Marissa said. "I prefer to skip the bread and fill up on the protein."

Ayla offered her a grateful smile and rolled a piece of cheese into a slice of turkey meat. "Do you have a job outside the ranch?"

"Yes. I work from home, so that allows me to care for the animals. Another reason this place functions so well for Becky and me."

When Marissa didn't offer more information about her job, Ayla took the hint that she didn't want to talk about it. "Thank you for opening your home to us."

"Are you kidding? I love the company. Been talking to myself and the horses too long."

Ayla laughed. "I did the same thing. My only company for the past six months has been a gelatin ballistics mannequin I named George."

Marissa chortled. "You win. That's worse."

"Right?" Ayla took another bite. The tension lessened, and she felt herself relaxing under Marissa's presence.

"I assume Commander Beckham updated you?" Chance said.

Ayla hated talking about the seriousness of her situation, but Marissa deserved advance notice of the danger they faced.

"He has. I worked too long in the military, so I don't require unnecessary details."

"I understand if you're uncomfortable with us being here." Ayla hoped Marissa didn't take her up on the offer to bail.

"Are you kidding? I've faced worse than a bunch of hoodlum gang members." She bit into a strawberry. "But we'll also be smart. Never underestimate your enemy."

"Ezra said that all the time." The familiar sadness pressed in on her.

They finished eating their meal, discussing lighter topics and listening to Marissa's stories of her time overseas. The woman amazed Ayla. She was beautiful and fearless.

"I want to be you when I grow up," Ayla halfway joked as she did the lunch dishes.

Marissa guffawed. "Oh, sister, set your dreams higher than on little old me."

"Seriously, though, thank you for letting us stay here. It's like a paradise."

Chance leaned against the wall. "She's right. You might never get rid of us."

"Ha. Now that I've got you bamboozled, let's head out to the pasture and bring in the horses. If cleaning stalls doesn't change your mind, you're welcome to stay."

Ayla grinned.

Marissa glanced at Ayla's clothing. "There are work boots and jeans in the closet. You'll need those."

Ayla hurried to the bedroom, quickly locating the clothing, and changed. She glanced at herself in the mirror. "I could get used to this." The jeans fit her well, and though the boots were a little large, an extra pair of socks took care of that problem. She joined Marissa and Chance outside.

Marissa sat atop Shad ready to go. "I'll round them up, and they'll come to the gate. When they do, Chance, help guide them into the stalls. They're trained and they'll follow you."

"Got it."

They watched as she rode out to the far side of the pasture. Four of the horses stood together, their tails swishing away unwanted flies.

"I'd rather do that," Chance mumbled.

"It's better than dodging shooters," Ayla contended. But how long would that last?

Chance's burner cell phone rang, jolting him awake. He winced from the ache in his muscles as he reached to answer it. Morning light burst through the window, and the aromas of bacon and coffee wafted to him. A glance at the alarm clock told him it was 8:02. Chance bolted upright. How had he slept so long? A second ring had him answering with a croaked "Hello?"

"Did some digging around on Octavia Warden," Walsh said in greeting. "She's been out of town since the funeral but had a flight into Des Moines last evening."

"Were there any threats against Octavia's life?" Chance rubbed the sleep from his eyes. On her cot, Destiny yawned, emitting a squeaking sound, and stretching her legs, flexing her paws. Clearly, he wasn't the only tired one.

"No. But with RJ dead, there was no reason for them to harm Octavia. She couldn't be used as a bargaining chip and claimed no knowledge of the list," Walsh replied.

"Ayla assumed the same thing."

"Keep me updated," Walsh said, disconnecting.

Chance looked at the phone. "Guess he doesn't say goodbye, either," he muttered sarcastically.

Destiny got to her feet, leaning her head on the bed.

"I'm up, let's go." He threw his legs over the edge and tugged on a clean pair of cargo pants.

Three raps on the door just as he reached for it startled him. He tugged it open, and Ayla stepped back, both hands wrapped around a coffee mug. "I didn't expect you to respond so quickly."

He grinned. "Sorry, Walsh already provided a wake-up call."

"Breakfast is ready," Ayla said. "I'll take Destiny out if you want to use the bathroom."

"Thanks, I'll be out in just a second." Chance shuffled to the bathroom and closed the door.

By the time he got to the dining table, Marissa and Ayla had a full spread laid out.

"Welcome to the land of the living," Marissa teased.

He groaned. "Sorry, I thought I set the alarm."

"Oh, the alarm doesn't work." Marissa loaded her plate with scrambled eggs.

"Well, that explains everything." Chance chuckled, pouring a cup of coffee from the carafe on the table.

"I slept like a rock," Ayla said.

"I'm glad to hear it. Although I suspect the hard labor contributed to the exhaustion."

Chance winced, lifting his achy arm to reach for the bacon. "I've had CrossFit workouts that affected me less."

Marissa laughed. "Becky will love hearing that."

Their forks clinked on the plates as each consumed the delicious offerings.

"I hate to bring shop talk to the table," Chance told Ayla, "But Commander Walsh called this morning."

Marissa began cleaning up the dishes. "You two sit. I'll get out of your hair."

Chance relayed Walsh's update.

"Hmm, I'm glad Octavia is okay," Ayla said. "I keep pondering the phrase 'you'll know George.'"

"Yeah, the team is focused there, too."

"We used George for training. Mostly shooting scenarios, though."

"Your guess is as good as mine. The bigger factor is finding the list. Clearly Sutler will do whatever it takes. Considering it holds the names of officials working in every level of government, not to mention the judicial and justice systems, he's got powerful people under his control who can't afford for word to get out that they're corrupt. Many people would end up in jail."

"Why would RJ have the list?"

"Do you really want me to answer that?" Chance sighed, leaning forward, both hands wrapped around the coffee mug. "Ayla, I wish I could say your boss was this super-upstanding guy, but Sutler went after him for a reason. So, he either worked with EastSide7 or they were recruiting him."

"I don't want to believe that."

Something in her reply left Chance wondering. What was she hiding? He tried a different approach. "Maybe he worked with the gang and wanted out. He could have been using the list as leverage to escape."

Ayla seemed to consider his words. "I hate that option."

"But it's not impossible."

Ayla sighed. "No. You didn't know him like I did."

"Exactly. You can offer something to this investigation that we can't. No amount of digging into the judge's past behavior will tell us what you experienced day in and day out with him."

Ayla averted her gaze. "I think RJ had the list because he never denied it to Myles."

"If that's true, he might've hidden it."

Ayla blinked. "Wait. Octavia is in danger."

"Negative. Walsh said she's had no death threats."

"She's been away since the funeral." Ayla pushed back from the table. "If RJ hid the list at the house, Myles might go there to look for it."

"But why wait until now? Besides, he's had the means to search for her all this time."

"We need to check on her and make sure she's okay."

Chance shook his head. "No. We'll send the team."

"Fine, ask for backup, but, Chance, we must talk to her. She might tell us something she wouldn't tell law enforcement. Remember, she's no fan." Ayla continued, "I left my phone in my bedroom." She held out her hand. "Can I borrow yours? I'll call her."

Chance gave a disapproving frown while passing her the phone then poured a second cup of coffee.

Ayla dialed, but after several seconds, she set it down. "No one answered. Something is wrong."

"Don't jump to conclusions. You said yourself Judge Warden didn't answer his phone."

"That was RJ, not Octavia."

"I'll send the team." Chance reached for the phone.

"She won't talk to them." Ayla's green eyes probed his. "Please, Chance, I'm worried."

"I'll ask Walsh to meet us there this afternoon."

She pressed a hand to his arm. "No. Now."

Walsh assured Chance they'd have backup units meet them at the house. Annoyed, but without a viable argument not to go, Chance drove Ayla to Octavia's Des Moines house.

She's never been super forthcoming. Ayla might get something out of her to help with the investigation. Chance replayed Walsh's words in his mind.

Since her husband's murder, Octavia had remained out of state without any incident or attack, therefore, in his estimation, she wasn't a target. That brought on more curiosity. Why wouldn't the gang try to go after the person closest to the judge?

"You're quiet," Ayla said.

"Have a lot on my mind. I want to handle this in a way that will be beneficial to the case."

"The police questioned Octavia on multiple occasions."

"True, and she never offered anything helpful."

"We're not going there to interrogate her," Ayla said.

Chance didn't reply.

"Are we?" Ayla shifted in her seat to face him, defensiveness rising in her tone. "Chance, she's innocent in the whole mess. She wasn't even home when Myles killed RJ."

Why did Ayla feel compelled to defend the Wardens? "But she might have information about the list."

"No way. She doesn't like cops, but she'd not withhold information pertinent to the case."

"If she was aware she possessed the knowledge. If the judge hid the list, he might've used normal parts of his day or routine types of things. For instance, suppose he golfed. He could've put it in his golf bag."

"RJ didn't golf."

Once more with defending the corrupt judge. Nobody had access to EastSide7 accidentally. Chance fought the urge to roll his eyes. "It's a hypothetical assumption. At times, people possess information unknowingly. Octavia might not realize something is worth telling us."

"I won't deceive her."

"I'm not asking you to do anything dishonest. Just engage her in normal conversation."

She shot him a wary glance. "Fine. But I'm telling you, Octavia was devastated over RJ's murder. She'd want Myles in jail."

"Ayla, this is part of the investigation. Finding the list is the beginning of the end of this nightmare for you. Remember that."

Ayla sighed and faced the windshield. "Just…be nice to her. Octavia exudes a tough exterior, but she's a sweet lady."

"I'm not going to tie her to a chair with a bright light shining in her eyes."

"Good to know." Perched on the end of her seat, she pointed to the largest home on the block. "That's the place."

The audaciousness of Judge Warden's Des Moines' home shouldn't have surprised Chance, especially after seeing Commander Beckham's horse ranch. Something about the home, nothing short of a mansion, added to Chance's low opinion of the judge. Surely, RJ Warden had worked with EastSide7, allowing him to fund his lifestyle with drug and blood money. The area's elaborate houses built in the early 1900s were highly valued properties positioned on older, narrow streets, with alleys separating the backyards.

He pulled up and parked in the driveway. All four garage doors were closed. Chance's cell rang. Walsh. "Sir."

"Backup is delayed due to a multi-jurisdictional incident."

"Roger that."

"Only proceed with the Warden interview if you feel comfortable doing so."

"Okay." They disconnected. "We don't have backup."

"Maybe we won't need it."

Before Chance had removed his seat belt, Ayla was out of the vehicle and headed up the front porch steps. "We'll be right behind you," he mumbled sarcastically, shutting off the engine. Chance threw open his door. "Ayla, wait!"

They needed to be cautious about how they approached Octavia. To her credit, Ayla paused, hand on her hip.

Chance released Destiny from her kennel and snapped on her leash. The duo joined Ayla, and they hurried up the winding sidewalk to the porch just as the front door whipped open. Chance's hand instinctively moved to his gun.

A fifty-something woman appeared in the doorway and stepped outside, pausing in midstride, her mouth agape but unspeaking. She blinked, wide-eyed, then rushed toward them, arms outstretched. "Ayla!"

Chance shifted closer, making his presence known and moving protectively in front of Ayla.

Octavia's posture stiffened, scrutinizing him with the disdain of an exterminator staring down an insect. "Who are you?"

Ayla must've sensed the change because she said, "This is Deputy US Marshal Chance Tavalla and his K-9, Destiny."

Octavia's smile flat lined across her lips. The expression had never reached her eyes, which remained cold and fixed on Chance. "You're a cop?"

He removed his sunglasses and extended a hand. "I'm with the Heartland Fugitive Task Force."

"He's helping with RJ's case," Ayla explained.

"A cop."

"Deputy US Marshal," he corrected.

Octavia rolled her eyes. "Same difference. I haven't even had a chance to call the authorities, but since you're here, you can work the scene."

Ayla and Chance exchanged confused looks.

"Beg your pardon?" he asked. "What scene?"

"Never mind." Octavia spun on her high-heeled pumps and made her way up the steps. "Well, come on."

Ayla took the lead with Chance and Destiny trailing. She stopped abruptly in the foyer, forcing Chance to peer around her through the archway that led to the living room. Porcelain and glass shards littered the thick white carpet. The intruders had dissected the couch cushions, which lay spewing their innards.

Chance touched Ayla's shoulder. "Stay here and let us clear the house."

Octavia pushed past him. "Surely they'd have attacked us by now if they were still here."

"That depends on whether they're searching for you or something else," Chance retorted.

Octavia's glare traveled to Destiny. "That filthy creature is not allowed inside."

The shepherd nudged Chance's hand and quirked a furry eyebrow. "My partner goes where I go."

Ayla placed a hand on Octavia's shoulder. "He's only doing his job."

"Yes, of course." Octavia's harsh demeanor softened slightly, but the coldness in her eyes remained. "Fine, proceed."

"Did you notice any signs of forced entry?" He unholstered his weapon.

"I haven't had the opportunity to look. I just walked in through the garage door and saw this prior to your arrival." She gestured with one hand, extending her perfectly manicured fingers toward the mess.

Chance released Destiny from her leash and commanded, "Hunt."

Together, the duo cautiously surveyed the elaborate

home. The Wardens had renovated the 1930s Victorian to include an updated kitchen complete with the finest appliances. The same was true of all three bathrooms on the upper level. Decorative wood carvings enhanced the banister railing, and white carpet spanned the floors, with hardwood borders peeking at the edges.

Chance holstered his gun as he and Destiny returned to the foyer where Ayla and Octavia waited, speaking in soft tones. "Did you call the police?"

"No, I arrived just prior to you."

"Wasn't your flight last evening?" Chance kept his tone light and conversational.

"Why are you checking up on me?" Octavia narrowed her eyes as she looked at him.

"I asked him to. I was worried," Ayla defended.

Octavia patted her hand. "Oh, dear, you needn't worry about me. Inclement weather in Washington canceled my flight, which forced me to stay in a pit of a hotel until today." She brushed her skirt as though emphasizing her tragedy, but her immaculate appearance voided that complaint.

"That's why you didn't answer your phone." Chance jerked his chin at Ayla in an I-told-you-so gesture. She rolled her eyes in response.

"Yes." Octavia walked past him, her heels tapping softly in the entry then growing silent as she entered the living room. "The audacity of some criminal invading my marital home! Losing my husband devastated me. Now, I return to find this mess." She moved to a floral wing-back chair and dropped onto the cushion.

"Do you have any idea who would've done this?" Ayla asked her.

"That awful EastSide7. But why are they bothering me?"

"Good question," Chance replied. "You've had no threats since your husband's death?"

"Murder, Officer. His death wasn't due to natural causes. Myles Sutler struck down my sweet RJ!" Octavia burst into tears, her last words rising in a crescendo to match her emotions.

Ayla glowered at him and rushed to her, kneeling in front of the older woman and holding her hands. "Are you okay?"

She nodded, though her coiffed hair didn't budge. "Yes."

"Did anyone have access to your home?" Chance prepared for the woman's attack.

"Yes." Octavia exhaled with the impatience of speaking to a child. "My housekeeper comes three times a week. She called this morning requesting a day off tomorrow."

"So, whoever broke in here used another method of entry," Ayla replied.

Chance walked to the French doors at the far side of the dining room. Both were locked and secured. He continued his perusal, Ayla and Octavia's conversation unintelligible from where he stood. He located a window in the family room at the back side of the house and noticed it was closed but unlocked. "Aha," he said softly, gaining Destiny's attention. She paused and tilted her head. "We found the most likely point of entry."

Destiny *mrffed* and trailed him to the dining room. "Octavia, it's unsafe for you to stay here."

She stopped speaking and faced him. With one hand, she swiped at a nonexistent tear on her cheek. "Excuse me?"

"It's not safe," Ayla repeated.

Destiny turned and faced the living room, separated by the hallway. She barked and emitted a low growl. Chance reached for his weapon. "Stay down."

Octavia gasped as Ayla tugged her down to the carpet.

Chance motioned for Destiny, leashing her, and they moved to the kitchen.

Gunfire erupted from outside.

"Stay down!" Chance hollered, making his way to the living room.

Rapid fire, indicating more than one shooter wielding automatic weapons, mutilated the Warden house. Chance checked his magazine. Not enough firepower to combat multiple assailants.

Shots circled them from all sides. They were surrounded.

SIX

Octavia's piercing screams rivaled the rapid gunfire, and it occurred to Ayla that the sound no longer terrified her. When had that happened? They remained crouched behind the sofa, both with their arms wrapped over their heads to guard against the spraying debris. Then, as quickly as it began, the shots ceased, and the screeching of tires implied the shooters had fled.

Ayla peered around the back side of the sofa, spotting Chance as he ran to the window and confirmed, "They're gone."

She barely heard him over Octavia's panicked cries. Ayla placed a hand on the woman's shoulder, startling her. "It's over."

She lifted her gaze, meeting Ayla's eyes. "What's happening?" Octavia cried. "Why is someone doing this to me?"

"It's not about you. They want me dead," Ayla said, her voice dull, as if she'd accepted the reality.

"Oh, honey." Octavia pulled Ayla into her arms in a strange and out-of-character display of affection. She held Ayla with the tenderness of a parent. "I'm so sorry for all this has done to you."

Tears welled, but Ayla blinked them away, unwilling to surrender to self-pity. *Warriors don't weep until after they win the battle.* Once again, Ezra's words invaded the moment. Now wasn't the time to fall apart. Instead, she focused her empathy on Octavia. The incident no doubt fell beyond her emotional repertoire, whereas serving as EastSide7's target had desensitized Ayla. Only numbness lingered, along with the inescapable urge to wake from the never-ending nightmare.

Destiny nudged Ayla's hand, and she released herself from Octavia's hold to stroke the animal's soft muzzle.

"Are you both okay?" Chance stood beside her and extended a hand, helping Ayla then Octavia to their feet.

"Of course not!" Octavia snarled, returning to her less approachable self.

"We have to get out of here," he replied.

"But Ayla said they're after her." Octavia's cold reply oozed insensitivity as she brushed off her pencil skirt. She stormed to the window, gaping at the damage.

"Probably," Chance concurred, "but let's play it safe. Please move away from the windows while I call the team."

"We'll get Octavia's things together," Ayla reassured.

"Absolutely not!" Octavia barked, stomping around the room and picking up remnants of her expensive decor. She held shattered porcelain from her vases in both hands and turned in a circle, as though bewildered by what to do with them. "Look at what these maniacs have done to my home! This is unacceptable. You should've stopped them! Why didn't you do something? Isn't your *dog* supposed to be telling us to watch out for these attacks? What good are you?"

Chance paused, his expression flickering between befuddlement and anger on his handsome face.

Ayla was used to Octavia's mood swings and angry tirades. "Make your calls." She turned her back to Octavia and rolled her eyes. Chance merely nodded. "Let's move to the kitchen." She gently took the woman's arm, expecting her to object.

Instead, she complied, and they transitioned into the airy kitchen, passing a large portrait of Octavia and RJ hanging on the wall. Bitterness tainted with betrayal coursed through her at the sight of the man she'd loved and admired her entire life.

She shook it off, allowing Octavia to enter the kitchen first. The woman never cooked, but she demanded the best of everything, and the house showed her expensive taste. She slid onto a high-backed stool at the breakfast bar, and Ayla moved to the refrigerator, both silently falling into their hierarchy roles.

"Let me get you something to drink."

"Thank you, dear."

Ayla withdrew two cans of sparkling water from the refrigerator and a glass for Octavia since she never drank directly from the aluminum. Once she'd passed the drink to Octavia, she popped the lid on her can and sipped the fizzing liquid.

"I miss him," Octavia said.

The unbidden comment surprised Ayla, and she fought not to choke on her drink. They hadn't talked about RJ since the funeral. She leaned against the counter. "I do, too. The time with him feels like eons ago."

"It does, doesn't it?" Octavia glanced up. "I can't figure out when my life became this mess."

"Right?" Ayla's life had plummeted into an inescapable rabbit hole six months ago, and at the rate things were going, that might never change. Unless they found the list. And Myles Sutler.

She surveyed the kitchen that had endured three interior decorator remodels, yet behind the pantry door, Ayla and her brother, Boyd's height charts remained undisturbed.

They'd grown up in the Warden house, completely unaware of the secrets hidden within its walls. RJ and Ayla's father's childhood friendship had grown, and since the Wardens had no children, they'd embraced Ayla and Boyd as their own.

Octavia's voice rose, dragging Ayla back to their conversation. "—never lived such an unpredictable and interrupted existence. I stayed away for fear something like today would happen. And sure enough, it did."

"I understand."

"You really do, don't you, sweetie?" Octavia tilted her head and reached across the counter. "I'm truly sorry for all you've endured. What can I do to help you?"

Chance's voice diverted her attention as he paced the area near the kitchen. Ayla caught bits and pieces of his conversation, confirming he was still on the phone with his team.

The weight of Octavia's gaze forced Ayla to respond. "Thank you, but Chance and his team have it under control."

Octavia snorted. "Hardly."

"It isn't safe for you to stay here," Ayla said.

"Why? If they're after you, they'll leave me alone."

"That's my assumption, but today could've ended badly for you."

Octavia raised her chin, resembling an obstinate child. "I'm not afraid."

The comment would've been comical under any other circumstances, but Ayla determined not to bring up the fact that they'd just crouched on the floor of her living room floor while Octavia had screamed.

Chance entered the room. "The team will be here to work the scene with the authorities."

"Oh, then I need to go clean up the mess." Octavia pushed away from the counter.

"You can't touch the scene until they're finished," he said.

As though he'd slapped her across the face, Octavia's head whipped back. "This is *my* house. I'll do whatever I like."

"HFTF might find evidence to help catch whoever shot at us," Ayla reminded her. Why was she acting so strangely? She was an educated woman and knew better.

"In the meantime, Commander Walsh ordered me to escort you to a safe house," Chance added.

"I will not leave my home." Octavia's tone didn't quite match her posture, arms folded over her chest in a defiant pose.

"We could arrange a protection detail with the local PD or marshals," Chance offered.

Octavia snorted. "Wasn't Ayla in witness protection? Why is she here now? Aren't you supposed to protect her? I hardly see how that'll solve any problems."

Ayla winced and mouthed *sorry* from behind Octavia. Chance's cheeks morphed into a bright blush, and he flicked a glance upward. "EastSide7 vandalized your house before we arrived."

Ayla noticed he didn't specifically mention the list, though it wasn't news to Octavia. She was aware of the details, and law enforcement had questioned her at length.

"Don't be coy. I know what you're implying. And before you ask, no, I don't know where the list is!" Octavia shot back. "And I don't believe RJ had it."

"How can you be certain?" Chance stood with his feet shoulder width apart, arms crossed. He wore a strong and unyielding expression.

"I've answered these questions months ago, but for the

sake of argument, I'll tell you again, as it's apparent none of you share information." Octavia busied herself wiping the spotless kitchen counter a little too vigorously. "RJ was a good man. He would not possess that corrupt list."

"Unless he was on it."

Ayla shot Chance a glare that she hoped conveyed her irritation at his comment. He didn't waver.

"Officer Tavalla—" Octavia began.

"Deputy US Marshal Tavalla," Chance corrected in an unmistakable steely tone.

They continued debating, and Ayla studied the woman who had always exhibited a composed and rational exterior. Professional, stiff and not overly emotional, Octavia still had always been kind to Ayla. If only Chance saw that side of her. Their arguing intensified until they were yelling, and Ayla gripped the counter to keep from fleeing the room. She had to intervene, since the two were incapable of civil communication.

"Listen, Octavia, you're in danger. Please let Chance and his team protect you. Those creeps might be back, and they could get more violent," Ayla pleaded.

Octavia faced her, and for the first time, fear glistened in her cold, unyielding eyes.

"It's not an option," Chance said, impatience in his tone.

"Thank you, but no. Until I came back here, I had no death threats or issues."

Ayla tried again, placing a hand on Octavia's arm, and the muscle stiffened beneath the silk blouse sleeve. "Please."

Her expression softened. "Fine. If the gang wants this place, let them have it. But I'm not moving to some safe house." She snorted. "Which will be anything but. I'll head to my cousin's home on the East Coast. She's already offered me the summer cottage in South Carolina as a place to stay until this all blows over."

Chance worked his jaw. "This isn't a dispute over flowers. Anyone involved in this case is in danger until we locate the list and apprehend all those involved."

"That's inconsequential to me. If I had any inclination where that list was, I'd gladly hand it over. It means nothing to me." Octavia sighed and dropped onto the stool, exhaustion apparent in her slumped shoulders. The fight seemed to have left her body as she said, "However, there is something I didn't tell the authorities. The day Myles Sutler killed RJ wasn't their first interaction."

"What do you mean?" Ayla joined her at the breakfast bar.

Octavia shot her a wary glance, wrapping both hands around the sparkling water glass. "Myles and his EastSide7 cronies approached my sweet RJ on multiple occasions."

"Why didn't you tell this to the authorities?" Chance asked.

Ayla shot him a look to back off before he upset Octavia again. They couldn't risk her shutting down the conversation. "Anything you share might help."

She patted Ayla's hand. "I didn't want you to see RJ in a poor light. He was a good man. They tried bribing him, threatening him and me, our livelihood and home. I begged him to just give them what they wanted. RJ was honorable and never relented."

Ayla stiffened, forcing her hands into her lap to keep them from shaking. She appreciated and loved RJ as an uncle, but he was hardly the saint Octavia painted him to be. He'd deceived those closest to him. Until Ayla discovered the truth, she, too, had placed him on a pedestal.

"RJ died because he was an honorable man," Octavia said. "He did the right thing. No good deed goes unpunished. Isn't that the cliché? RJ did not deserve what happened to him." Octavia turned to Ayla, and she struggled not to wilt under the woman's gaze.

Was she implying Ayla was at fault? That she should've prevented RJ's death by not stopping at the house that night? Ayla's mouth went dry, and she twisted her fingers, grounding herself.

Would Octavia sing her husband's praises if she knew the truth? The war Ayla fought within herself, between wanting to remember RJ as the kind and wonderful man who treated her as a niece, who was a friend to her family, whom she'd trusted and adored her entire adult life, combated with the RJ who had hurt her, lied, concealed the truth for decades and left her with the betrayal that wounded so deeply she couldn't bear the secret she held.

Raps on the front door provided Chance the opportunity to escape before he said anything he'd regret. "That's my team," he said, excusing himself from the kitchen.

Tiandra and Bosco's arrival brought relief. If he had to spend one more minute with Octavia Warden, he might come unglued. "Just in time." Chance closed the door.

Ayla stepped forward. "Bosco, right?" She gestured at the K-9 sniffing Destiny in greeting.

"I'm impressed you remembered," Tiandra commented, "especially after that slam course at the hotel."

"Mind if I pet him?" Ayla asked.

"Not at all." Tiandra gave a slight tug to the leash, and Bosco dropped to a sit.

Octavia approached, hesitating from a distance.

Chance prayed she didn't have a conniption fit because she had two *filthy beasts*, as she'd offensively referred to the K-9s, in her house.

Tiandra took a step forward, extending her hand. "Hi there, I'm FBI agent Tiandra Daugherty."

Octavia received the gesture with an icy, forced grin. Her eyes remained on Bosco. The Belgian Malinois offered a confident and unwavering stance that seemed to dare Octavia to approach. "Nice to meet you. I'm Octavia Warden."

"We'll work out the details with the authorities. Chance and Ayla, y'all need to leave. I'll escort Mrs. Warden when the cavalry arrives." Tiandra's instruction left no room for argument. "They're right behind me."

"We'll wait until the scene is secured," Chance said.

"Negative," Tiandra countered. "I'll contact you when the report is finished, but Walsh is adamant y'all get out of here."

As if to emphasize her command, sirens screamed in the distance.

"Octavia, please notify the team when you reach your destination." Ayla drew the woman into a quick hug then spun on her heel. "Let's go."

"Chance, you'll have to take my ride." No doubt his was riddled with bullet holes from the earlier barrage. "Here are the keys. Now trade me remotes," Tiandra said.

Ayla turned, sporting a quizzical expression.

Chance caught the keys Tiandra tossed him and exchanged the remote from his belt with hers. Then they went outside to Tiandra's vehicle.

Ayla had her seat belt secured by the time Chance finished loading Destiny into the dog kennel. He slid behind the wheel and started the engine.

The sirens were within a block by the time they turned off Octavia's street.

"What remote did you exchange with Tiandra?" Ayla asked.

"It allows me to open Destiny's kennel remotely in emergency situations," Chance replied.

"That's a pretty cool feature."

Destiny popped her head through the divider. "She thinks so, too," Chance said with a grin.

Ayla stroked the dog's head, but she grew quiet, and Chance didn't push her. The expedited exit left Chance a little bewildered, but communicating with women had never been his strength. Though the concept wasn't new for him, he'd accepted this truth in eighth grade when Delia Anders tossed a slushy into his lap when he asked if she'd set him up with her best friend. However, the interaction with Ayla and Octavia reminded him of his failures and the urgency of hunting fugitives, not babysitting witnesses.

Unable to come up with anything to chitchat about, Chance focused on the road and the case. Ayla twisted in her seat, staring out the window. The commute remained relatively quiet, and after a half hour, Chance realized something had affected Ayla. She'd not spoken beyond single-word answers to any of the questions he'd struggled to ask.

"You're awfully quiet. Did Octavia Warden upset you?" He'd tried numerous times to get Ayla talking. So far, nothing had proven effective. "She's hard to talk to, but you seem to have a way of getting through to her."

Ayla gave a one-shoulder shrug. "I've known her a long time."

He'd take the short sentence as a win. "Have you met the cousin in South Carolina she mentioned?"

"No. She's a private person. Until today, I wasn't aware she had family on the East Coast." Ayla twisted to face him. A noncommittal move that indicated she'd turn her back on him again, but he'd take the mini reprieve. "The attack was intended for me."

Chance sighed, running his hands over the steering wheel. "Possibly, but they'd ransacked the house prior. Yet it's strange she hasn't been a target all this time," he added. "Still, it's better for her to stay with her family just in case."

"EastSide7 doesn't care who they hurt. Octavia's experienced such pain. I put her life in danger going there. I should've listened to you."

"As much as I love being right—" Chance grinned but Ayla didn't respond. "You were concerned for her safety."

Ayla glanced down, her long lashes shadowing her emerald eyes. "What kind of people kill innocents to get what they want?"

"You don't want me to answer that."

"Sadly, I'm aware, and I'm tired of being the reason others are in danger."

"None of this is your fault."

Ayla snorted. "Right."

Great. He'd upset her again. Proof that communication wasn't his forte. He'd be single the rest of his life at the rate he was going.

Single? The idea smacked him. Since when was he cognizant of his relationship status? Chance shook off the ill-timed thought and considered the case.

In the short conference call with the team, they'd agreed Sutler was escalating in his efforts. Those on the list would increase the pressure for him to locate it. Good. The only concern for HFTF was what extremes he'd go to in order to reach Ayla. Interestingly, no one could say for sure if the attack had been targeting Ayla or Octavia.

Ayla's concerns for Octavia's safety might've been valid. Though Walsh had not apologized for agreeing to let Chance and Ayla travel to the Warden home—which would be out of character for him anyway, based on their prior interactions—he'd commented they'd never should've left the horse ranch. Still, the attack reinforced the team's belief that Sutler had an insider.

"What will they do with your truck?" Ayla asked, dragging him from the thoughts.

"Thanks to EastSide7's fine shooting abilities, it'll no doubt be totaled, and they'll have to issue me a new vehicle." Chance considered his bullet-ridden pickup and tightened his grip on the steering wheel. The K-9 vehicle was designed with temperature control settings especially devised to protect Destiny. Replacing the truck was expensive and took time, two things working against Chance with the team. Would they view him as costing them more than he was worth?

Ayla continued. "It was nice of Tiandra to loan her vehicle to us."

"Yeah, she's great." Chance sighed. "She's an exceptional handler, too. She taught me a lot with Destiny."

At the mention of her name, his German shepherd appeared through the divider. He reached up to stroke her fur, meeting Ayla's hand in the process and startling at the smoothness of her skin. He jerked back. "Sorry about that."

A soft blush covered her cheeks. "My bad. I should've asked first."

He glanced at his dog, who lay with her head on the console, eyes closed in appreciation of Ayla's touch.

"Destiny doesn't mind." Chance chuckled.

"She's so sweet."

"Ah, don't let her gentle demeanor fool you. If you were a criminal, she'd show you her strengths without fail."

Destiny popped one eye open at Chance as if to say, *really, you had to go there?*

"I have no doubt. She's got many talents," Ayla cooed to the dog. "When this is over, maybe I'll rescue a dog from the shelter. I'd enjoy having a companion and protector."

"I'm a huge advocate of rescuing animals, and dogs are a great deterrent for criminals. If given the option, they'll opt for a house without a bark warning system." And now he sounded like a commercial for the humane society.

Walsh had tasked him with getting to the root of Ayla's relationship with RJ and Octavia in the hopes of locating the list. Understanding their habits, vacations, etc. might lead to where he'd hidden it. Considering Chance's lack of conversation skills, he hadn't figured out a good way to approach the topic with Ayla without offending her.

"That settles it," Ayla said, "a dog it is."

Destiny sighed, eliciting a chuckle from her human companions.

"She agrees." He needed to get more information from Ayla, and that wouldn't happen with surface-level conversation. Despite his gut telling him to just leave it alone, he said, "I must ask. Are you really okay?" Not a great lead-in, but he'd struggled to find a question that kept her defenses low.

"Yes. I am." She turned away from him again. "I'm numb to the death threats by now."

Good going, Tavalla. Once more, you've ruined the moment. She'd talk about the case. So, if that's where they had to remain with their discussion, he'd take it over silence. "Without the list, I'm not sure where the team will start looking."

"They'll never find Myles." Ayla sighed and shifted in the seat. "He has too many connections and an army in EastSide7 willing to fight for him."

"Now, see, if I went into battle with that pessimism, the criminals would take over the world." Chance gave her a small smile, hoping to lighten her mood.

"Haven't they already done that?"

Sorrow hung in her voice, and empathy swarmed

Chance. He couldn't imagine the burden Ayla bore and the foreboding that would remain until the case was closed.

"You said you've known the judge and his wife a long time?"

"Yes. He and my father were childhood friends. They have no children. When my father passed away, RJ and Octavia stepped up to help my mother. Although Octavia doesn't possess motherly instincts. She's more like a rich, snobby aunt who tolerates us."

Chance grinned. "I'd agree that's an accurate description based on what I've seen. But I bet you were adorable."

The corners of her lips lifted, but a sadness hung in her green eyes. "Yeah, I guess I was kinda cute."

"Pigtails?"

"Always, with big bows."

"I only have a younger brother." He hated talking about himself or his family, but he needed to extend an olive branch of trust.

"Shelton, right?"

"Yes." That was all he was admitting. This investigation wasn't about Chance, it was about Ayla. "Did your mother get along with them?"

"Sort of, but she kept a distance." Ayla's tone indicated she meant to say more.

When she didn't continue, Chance pressed her. "Why?"

"I suppose she'd figured out something about them that we hadn't."

"Like?" The discussion was as difficult as extracting a molar.

"Who knows?" Ayla shrugged, but her demeanor said otherwise. What wasn't she sharing with him?

"You can trust me."

"Ha. That's a moving target, and really, nobody is trustworthy."

Chance reared back from the verbal slap, his defenses rising. "I realize we've only known each other a short time, but I think I've demonstrated I have your best interest at heart."

Ayla didn't look at him. "Everyone's got motives for doing things. No one works purely for altruistic reasons. You're here because you're forced to be. And solving this case would better your career. It's not as though you care about me."

Chance didn't reply for several seconds. She was right. "Wow. That's a bit of a jaded point of view."

"Yep. Life will do that to you."

He'd assumed they were making progress. What had occurred while he'd made the phone call that drastically changed Ayla's demeanor and attitude toward him? "What happened with Octavia that upset you? Or did I do something wrong?" *And if so, could you point out exactly what I said, since it's clear I'm clueless in how to talk to women?*

"I was reminded that no number of years totally reveals the truth about anyone. Family should protect each other, creating the foundation for our adult relationships. So, if you can't trust them, who does that leave?"

Ayla's words were a fresh stab to Chance's heart, dragging him back to memories of his younger self with Shelton running from bullying gang members. Ayla was right. He should've protected his little brother. That was an older sibling's one unspoken and expected job. Instead, he'd failed, and Shelton had paid the price every single day since.

By the time Chance pulled through the gate at the Walsh horse ranch, he'd gone through the full gamut of emotions. He parked inside the Morton building and shut off the engine, then faced her. "I disagree with you about family.

We all do the best we can, but expecting others to shield us from every bad thing is unrealistic."

"Maybe." She shrugged. "Or you've lived a naive or sheltered life."

"That's harsh, unfair and inaccurate on all counts."

Her green eyes flashed. "I'll never get involved with a man to the point of complete confidence in him."

How did she jump to that conclusion? "You must trust someone. Life is lonely." Not that Chance had personal experience with the former part of that statement. On the other hand, he was well acquainted with the latter half. He'd lived and would die alone.

She pinned him with a glower. "I've spent the past six months with only a gelatin ballistics mannequin to talk to. Still, I'd rather have that than get stabbed in the back."

Chance blinked. What was she implying? His defenses rose again. "Are you talking about RJ or someone else?" *Like me?*

"Anyone. I won't waste my life with someone who could turn around and betray me. What a slap in the face."

"That's a blanket statement that doesn't apply to every person."

"You're right, except I have yet to meet anyone who hasn't done that. Family should support and protect one another."

The circular conversation dragged him in directions he didn't want to go. But he needed Ayla to talk to him. "Ayla—" Chance reached for her. What was going on?

She shifted out of his reach. "I'm tired." She shoved open her door and stepped out, leaving Chance staring at her departing form.

"Lord, what just happened here?" He leaned back in the seat and stared at the ceiling, processing Ayla's words. *Family should protect one another.* Was she implying, as

Octavia had, that he was incapable of protecting her? The comment dug under his skin, pulling up the splinter of a memory again that he longed to forget.

He hadn't protected Shelton, and his brother had paid for Chance's ineptitude since the assault. Ayla's attacks had continued, and he'd failed to protect her and keep Sutler's men from finding them. She was right. He was incapable and he was stuck. Walsh wouldn't reassign him, so if he had any hope of continuing with the task force, he had to work with Ayla. How could he do that when she obviously despised him?

Destiny nudged his arm, and he stroked her ears, talking aloud. "That's the thing—I told Walsh to let us go fugitive hunting. I'm not capable of this witness babysitting job."

The shepherd gave a low *mrff.*

"See, you totally get it. Ayla's right, I can't protect her. And if she dies...if Sutler finds her...we'll lose our jobs." But that wasn't the only worry in Chance's mind, and Destiny again *mrffed* her understanding. "It's not just that. I mean it is, sort of. I like her. She's funny, beautiful, interesting and smart." Speaking the words, Chance realized losing Ayla had become his biggest fear. "I failed Shelton. What happens if I fail Ayla?"

If he failed, Ayla would die.

SEVEN

Ayla entered the house, her heart drumming hard against her chest as though she'd run a marathon. Chance had pushed for answers regarding RJ, and his questions had erupted her emotions unpredictably. She owed RJ no allegiance, yet Ayla couldn't bear to tell Chance the man she'd called Uncle wasn't honorable. He'd taken bribes before, so why not when Myles Sutler offered them? Or had he? Ayla sighed and slumped onto the large sofa. Why was she still defending RJ? Why did she continue to struggle with sharing the ugly truth with Chance?

Ayla sat on the sofa and leaned forward, resting her elbows against her knees, and put her head in her hands. She closed her eyes and replayed the conversation, realizing she'd spoken the words as though laying down a gauntlet. Did she want him to challenge her? Fight through her defenses?

No. That was ridiculous.

Chance's warning lingered, and she couldn't disagree. Unwillingness to trust anyone meant she'd never have a true relationship. The probability of a lonely existence saddened Ayla, weighing her down with the consequences.

She sat up straighter and got to her feet, catching a glimpse of a framed photo on a side table. Marissa and

Beckham stood together, smiling wide in front of three of the horses. She assumed they both did fine without spouses. Didn't they? What were their stories?

They'd taken charge of their future by building this beautiful ranch. She'd done the same by safeguarding her heart. No one like her father and RJ would blindside her with their lies and betrayals. Both were dead, leaving her without reconciliation or the opportunity for closure.

She made her way to the windows overlooking the pasture and barn, spotting Marissa with Shadow. She was fascinated by Marissa's interactions with the horse. They seemed to speak a silent language, engaged in a dance of mutual respect. Marissa's hand stroked the horse's muzzle as he rested his massive head on her shoulder. Though he was at least a foot taller than the woman, his gentle response proved his endearment to her. Ayla couldn't hear Marissa from where she stood, but Shadow seemed to hang on her every word.

Drawn to the pair, Ayla walked out the back door and made her way to them.

Marissa smiled as she neared. "I saw you guys pull up. Where are Chance and Destiny?"

"Um, I'm not sure." Ayla turned toward the Morton building, spotting no sign of either. "I was in the house for a little while." *After I stormed away from the poor, confused guy.*

A knowing look passed in Marissa's eyes. "How did the trip go?"

"You don't want to know," Ayla groused, hopping onto the fence rail.

"Try me." Shadow nudged Marissa, and she laughed. "Yes, I have treats for you."

Ayla gaped. "He knows when you have food in your pockets?"

"Yep, he's spoiled." She reached into her jacket. "Apple bites."

Ayla hopped down, and Marissa placed several small brown kidney-shaped objects in the center of her palm. "Hold your hand flat like this and let him take it."

The horse seemed to study her before grazing her hand with his lips then taking the treat. "He's so gentle."

"Yep. You can give him the others, too. It'll endear you to him forever."

Ayla loved the way he looked at her, with a tenderness and compassion she couldn't explain. When she'd finished feeding him, he nuzzled her hair, and she laughed.

"Shad, you're such a flirt. No more treats," Marissa chastised with a chuckle. "Let's take him inside for grooming."

Marissa gripped a lead rope and led the horse into the barn. After settling Shadow in his stall, she disappeared through a door at the back and returned carrying a large rectangular brush and comb. "Here ya go." She held out the brush.

Ayla stared at it before taking possession of the item. "What do I do?"

"I'll give you a crash course on grooming. Start with his mane, keeping one hand slowly moving along his body. That'll ground him to where you are. Your touch helps him not to startle. Do not walk behind him without your hand on his flank."

"I'll just stay where he can see me," Ayla replied.

"That works, too." Marissa snickered. "Takes time to build trust with them."

Trust. Using the brush, Ayla gently stroked the horse's neck. "Is this correct?"

Marissa nodded. "Yep, gently brush through his mane.

He'll tell you if he doesn't like something." With the long comb, she worked on the opposite side.

Shadow turned his head, his large dark eyes framed by the longest eyelashes Ayla had ever seen. The tension in her shoulders lessened. "He's peaceful."

"Horse therapy is the best kind. They read our emotions. If you're tense, it flows to them. So, you want to be calm, and somehow being around them helps do that." Marissa's tone was confident, soft, but firm.

"Are you scared to live out here by yourself?" Ayla ran the brush along the coarse hairs, gently working tangles free.

"Never. This place is my sanctuary, and the horses are the greatest friends you could ask for."

"It's easy to trust an animal. They won't betray you," Ayla blurted, but she found talking to Marissa easy. Especially because they couldn't see each other with the horse standing between them.

"Betray, no. But their survival instincts override everything. So, if they feel threatened, they respond to protect themselves."

Ayla considered the words. "I guess humans aren't that different."

"Not really. Trust is a precious thing. Easily broken and hard to fix once damaged."

"Exactly."

"Hardly impossible, though."

Shadow snorted softly, twisting to look at Marissa. "See, Shad agrees."

Ayla chuckled. "He does?"

"His prior owners mistreated him before we rescued Shad. It took a long time to build trust and even to get near him."

"How could anyone hurt such a beautiful creature?"

The idea tore at Ayla's heart. "He's so docile and sweet." She swept her hand across his velvety hide.

"Now. But he'd been hurt, and humans terrified him. It took patience, apple treats and a lot of effort before we saw results. The love came with a price. I broke my arm when he kicked me, not to mention the countless bruises in handling him."

"Why didn't you give up? I'd be afraid to go near him after all that."

"He didn't give up on me, either. Like any relationship, we had to work through our issues. And don't tell the others, but he's my favorite." Marissa reached up and stroked his neck. "Aren't you, handsome?"

Shadow gave a soft snort and bobbed his head, adding to the confirmation.

"Lately, trusting people has proven detrimental. The ones closest to me lied and betrayed me, then burdened me with their secrets." Why had she shared that?

"Yeah, secrets are strange. At their best, they're empowering, at their worst, devastating."

"Especially when they're not mine. I know things I don't want to know."

Marissa chuckled. "You've just described the military experience."

Ayla winced. "When you put it that way, I sound childish."

"Not at all. My dad used to say, the deeper you love, the greater your chance of experiencing pain. But you can't have the joy of loving them without that vulnerability."

Ayla stopped mid-brush. "Getting close and having someone hurt me again terrifies me."

"Only one way to fix that." Marissa moved around Shadow, coming face-to-face with Ayla. "You'll have to move to Antarctica."

"What?"

Humor danced in Marissa's cerulean eyes.

"Live in solitude without human contact. Where there are humans, pain exists. We're all fallible, sinful by nature. Even when we don't mean to hurt one another, we do it." Marissa stroked Shadow. "Like when I worked with this guy. He'd never hurt me intentionally, but he responded out of his own fears. There's a constant dance in relationships. We step on each other's toes and pray for forgiveness."

Ayla had lashed out at Chance. She'd distanced herself from her mother and brother, at first because she'd relished the independence, then after RJ's murder, she'd done so to protect them. That must've hurt them. She paused, fixated on Shadow's ebony body, shiny from the brushing that enhanced his beauty. "You're right."

"The key is what you do with the pain."

"I can't help my feelings."

"Emotions are normal, but we don't have to linger where they take us. No matter what others have done to you, you choose what to do with the fallout. Hold on to it and grow bitter and afraid, which leaves you isolated and miserable." Marissa moved around Shad's flank, working the comb through his long black tail. "Or let God heal those places and turn the pain for good. The way Shadow did. He let us work with him and restore the broken places. And in doing so, he has a forever home where we love and care for him beyond the atrocities he endured."

"But what if he'd gone somewhere worse? Or had permanently hurt you?"

"Definite possibilities. Guess we both took the risk. I'm grateful for every injury."

"Why?"

"He taught us how to handle others who are abused and mistreated. We've used his recovery to learn techniques for other horses in the same situation. He allowed his wounds to be turned for good. God wastes nothing. Not even pain. You make your own choices about how you'll treat others. None of us faces trials, pain and betrayal alone without God's powerful in-charge hand. He takes that mess and makes it a blessing. There're countless stories in the Bible of Him doing just that."

Ayla believed in God, and she'd grown up in the church. But reading the Bible on a Sunday morning and putting the principles into action like Marissa did were totally different.

Marissa continued, "Enduring the hard stuff makes us stronger, emotionally and physically. Same in military training. We're pushed way past our limits because that takes us to the next level. In the end, we do things beyond anything we dreamed possible."

Ayla tilted her head, running her fingers over the rough brush bristles. "You're brilliant and wise."

"Right? Tell my brother." Marissa made a silly face.

Ayla chuckled. "Can I ask a personal question?"

"Um, I gotta make a phone call." She playfully pretended to flee the building. "I'm only teasing. I'm an open book."

"Why aren't you married?"

"I almost was." A sadness passed over Marissa's playful expression. "I came home at the end of my tour after my fiancé was killed in action."

"Oh, I'm such a jerk. I'm so sorry!" Ayla pressed her hand against her throat. "I never should've asked."

"It's okay. Someday I'll tell you all about him."

Ayla looked down at the wooden floor. *Me and my big mouth.*

"Right now, I'm guessing you need to talk to Chance?"

Ayla shifted, one hand on her hip, and glanced around. "Do you have cameras or something?"

"Yes, but not for spying on potential couples."

"Couples?"

Marissa nodded. "I'm a keen observer, and watching the two of you, it's obvious there are sparks."

Ayla's ears warmed with embarrassment.

"Don't worry, I think the feeling is mutual."

"You do?"

"Absolutely. And one thing I can tell you for certain is my big brother has a gift for reading people. He brought Chance into the elite Heartland Fugitive Task Force because he recognizes his qualities. Becky won't risk his team's lives with anyone he can't trust."

"What if I'm wrong about him?" Ayla passed Marissa the brush.

"Then you'll learn something about yourself and build that muscle."

"He seems like a great guy," Ayla admitted.

"Um, yeah. And if the interior is as good as the exterior, I'd say you struck gold, sister." Marissa waggled her eyebrows, and Ayla laughed.

"Thank you for talking with me."

"Anytime. Just remember, love is worth the risk."

Ayla's throat tightened with emotion as she walked out of the barn. Immediately she spotted Chance and Destiny strolling along the path at the far side of the property.

Without hesitation, she hurried to catch up to them.

At her approach, Chance's hand flew to his gun. "What's wrong?"

Chance moved in front of Ayla, prepared to fire at any threat.

"Relax." Ayla smiled. "I just needed to talk to you."

Chance lowered his hand. "Okay." Ayla didn't move, and after several long silent seconds, he said, "It's beautiful out. How about a walk around the property?"

"That sounds great."

They strolled the lane, waving to Marissa working with the paint horse, Caesar.

Chance led the way from the lane through a grove, and they climbed the small hill to a pond encircled by trees.

"I can't get over how picturesque this place is," Ayla said.

"No kidding." He spotted a dock. "Let's head over there."

They strode through the grass. Dragonflies whizzed around them, perching on the cattails. Destiny chased a rabbit, giving up after a few feet.

Chance chuckled. "Making friends?"

The shepherd *mrffed* and trotted ahead.

"First, I'm sorry for snapping at you on the way back from Octavia's."

Grateful she started the conversation, Chance said, "I shouldn't have pushed."

"It's your job to ask questions. I was afraid to answer them."

He tilted his head. "Why?"

"You were right. The visit with Octavia activated some emotional trigger buttons for me."

They made their way onto the dock. A bullfrog croaked loudly from beneath the murky water. A mallard couple floated near the opposite side, occasionally diving, then lifting their heads to shake down the food they'd caught. Ayla placed her hands on the railing. A breeze fluttered her auburn hair, and he reached up, tucking a piece behind her ear, exposing a tiny silver stud earring. She glanced down, and everything within Chance wanted to pull her into his arms. Instead, he shoved his hands into his pockets and stepped back, creating space between them.

"Octavia said RJ was a good man who never accepted bribes," Ayla said. "That wasn't true."

He shifted and leaned against the railing, processing her words with a straight face so as not to portray his satisfaction for getting dirt on RJ. "He took bribes from Sutler?"

"Can't speak to that." Ayla stuffed her shaking hands into her pockets. "Before I blurt this confession, I need to give you some background."

"Okay." Now he was really confused.

"My dad was a good man who made some poor choices. It sounds like I'm defending him, and I probably am, but I want to establish he wasn't a criminal. His behavior was totally out of character."

"I understand." Though he didn't.

"Dad gambled and got himself in deep with dangerous loan sharks."

"How'd you find out?"

"I found documents in RJ's files right before Myles murdered him."

"Did you talk to the judge?"

Ayla glowered at him, and he realized he'd interrupted her.

"Never had the opportunity." She turned, walking off the dock.

Chance whistled for Destiny, who was sniffing along the pond.

"My father's employer charged him with embezzlement after his terminal cancer diagnosis. Apparently, our family was in dire straits. He gambled with the intention of helping us, so my mom didn't lose everything when he passed." She stopped walking. "After his arrest, he bribed his friend RJ to dismiss the charges, which he did."

"Wow." Chance ran his hand over his head.

"I understand why Dad did it. He'd messed up and was desperate to fix it before—" Ayla averted her gaze, not finishing the sentence. "So, he stole. He probably wouldn't have lived long enough to see the trial, but the conviction would've cost my mom everything. I'm convinced she's oblivious to what Dad did, and I want to keep it that way." She began walking again, and Chance kept pace beside her.

Was that what she'd meant about family protecting each other? "Finding the documents destroyed your memory of your father?"

They reached the path. Marissa wasn't in the pasture, and in the distance, the open barn door had him assuming she'd gone inside.

"In a way. I mean, I still have wonderful memories, and I'm not excusing his behavior or RJ's." Ayla shook her head. "Maybe I am." She leaned against the fence. "I trusted them both." Her eyes welled with tears.

Chance pulled her into his arms. The action felt natural and right until he smelled her shampoo and glanced down. The possible implications slammed into him. Still, he didn't let her go. "Thank you for entrusting this secret to me. I mistrusted Warden, but I wasn't sure why."

She withdrew from him, and he gave himself a mental slap upside the head. *Way to kill the moment, Tavalla.*

Ayla crossed her arms. "He wasn't a horrible man."

"I didn't know him as you did. We clashed at every interaction, so I have no other reference."

"I suppose that's true." She kicked at the ground, dislodging a small stone.

Chance studied the way her hair swept around her face, concealing her features. She'd always exuded confidence and strength when they'd spoken at the courthouse, but he saw that fading, and it worried him.

"Can I tell you a secret?"

The request surprised him. "You have my full attention."

She looked up, and the vulnerability she conveyed had him wanting to shield and protect her. And he had no business going there.

"I hate that my first reaction is to defend RJ." Ayla sighed. "I also don't like talking badly about anyone and hope others don't do that to me. I'm hypervigilant about it."

"That's normal when you care for someone."

"Or naive." She glanced down, and questions bombarded Chance. What did she mean? Who was she referring to?

"You are far from naive."

"I owe RJ so much. My dad passed away when I was twelve. RJ paid my college tuition, helped me choose my career. He gave me my first job and attended every dance recital and school event. Even those father-daughter things. He didn't have to do that."

No wonder she was protective of the judge. Chance's defenses lowered as he realized he'd viewed the man through his own perspective rather than listening to her. "I suppose it's my turn to confess. I wanted to share my concerns about the judge with you, but I didn't want to upset you." That wasn't entirely true. He figured she'd explode and go right into defending the egomaniac. What good would that do either of them? "I tried to keep my reservations to myself."

Ayla snorted with a sideways grin. "You should tell that to your face."

"Is it that bad?" He frowned.

She laughed. "Not lousy, but your expressions are descriptive."

"I was a jerk?" He winced.

She shrugged. "I didn't say that."

"It's okay. I know I was defensive with my own prejudices about Judge Warden."

"RJ was like my uncle, and I was always taught to protect family."

Chance nodded. He'd applied her words to himself when that hadn't been her intention at all.

Ayla tilted her head. "You've stumped me this time. What's that expression saying?"

"My face was talking again?" he asked, half-jokingly.

"Definitely."

"I had my own emotional triggers, but let's come back to that. Please continue." He also picked up on how she didn't reference Octavia in the same manner. Chance hesitated, and her gaze probed him to speak. "What about Octavia?"

Conflicting emotions swirled in Ayla's eyes, and she hesitated, as though trying to formulate her response.

"I'm sorry, it's really none of my business," he hurried to add. Except it was, because the team needed information about Judge Warden's life.

"Octavia is…complicated."

"Because?"

"She didn't come from money, but she hides it well. She's all about looks, possessions and appearances." Ayla shifted from one foot to another. "She never had a lot of patience for my brother and me. Kids weren't her strong suit." As though she needed to justify her response, she added, "But she wasn't mean to us or anything."

Ayla moved to the fence and climbed up on it. "Okay, your turn. Share your triggers. I'm all ears."

His gaze traveled over Ayla, taking in her green eyes, the curve of her cheek to her full lips. "Hardly." The blurted word escaped before he could stop it. In an effort to cover his misstep, Chance waggled his eyebrows teasingly, extracting a laugh from Ayla. The sound was amazing and somehow enhanced her attractiveness.

Chance didn't want the honest discussion to end, but old wounds rose within him. Once he revealed his past, she'd never look at him the same. Still, she'd trusted him with her secrets. The urge to reciprocate overrode his fears and he began his story. "I grew up in a rough part of town. Lots of gangs and violence."

Ayla watched him, waiting for him to continue.

"Mom was adamant Shelton and I stick together. Never go anywhere alone. Strength in numbers and all that. We were walking home from middle school when several gang members jumped us. We tried fighting back, but they outnumbered us. I should've protected Shelton better, but I couldn't reach him. They beat him up, and he lost sight in one eye." The memory overwhelmed him with sorrow.

"I'm so sorry!" Ayla put her hands over her mouth. "Were you hurt, too?"

"Nothing like Shelton's injuries. My folks were mortified, and we moved shortly after that. They were great, but they kept my failure to protect Shelton before me in little ways like not putting me in charge of him anymore. Or not allowing us to go anywhere without adult supervision. I don't think they meant it hurtfully, more as a caution for the future, but it affected me."

"I can't even imagine." Ayla placed both hands on the fence railing, bracing herself. "Shelton's okay now?"

"Yes, he's a high school history teacher."

"How did it affect your relationship with him?"

"It brought us closer, believe it or not. Shared trauma has that effect." Along with the guilt that kept Chance beholden to him. "I got into law enforcement because I want to take down people like Myles Sutler and EastSide7. Gangs who recruit kids who hurt other kids."

"You turned the hurt into something good."

"Never really thought of it that way. I figured it's more like revenge." Chance hesitated, unwilling to share the deeper part of the story. His emotional plagues and scars bred in fear that he'd never have what it took to protect someone. Fugitive hunting was his gift. But he botched protection detail.

"You've succeeded in your career," Ayla told him. "I feel safe with you. And that's saying a lot."

The look in her eyes, the kindness and understanding, filled a place in his heart that bolstered his confidence. What would she say if he told her of his inabilities? He couldn't bear to disappoint her or give her reason to think less of him.

Ayla hopped down and placed her hands on his forearms. Her touch sent a jolt through him. "I'm sorry for you and Shelton. Marissa and I talked about turning the pain we experienced into good. You're a perfect example. I'm grateful men like you fight for us. You're a hero."

Hardly. He was a wimp.

"Chance?" Ayla shifted her hand to his chin, lifting his gaze to meet hers.

"Thank you for all you've done to help me. You've saved my life multiple times, and I am forever grateful."

Lost in her presence, Chance leaned down, his face close to Ayla's. She let out a breath, a whisper of it meeting his cheek. Her long eyelashes fluttered. Heat between them warmed Chance. He slid his hand to the small of her back, and she melted into his embrace, stepping closer and lifting her head. Her lips parted slightly, and Chance moved closer, brushing a kiss against her mouth.

Destiny barked, shocking them, and they stepped apart, leaving the kiss incomplete.

Groaning in frustration, Chance surveyed the grounds for his dog. What had she found so compelling that she'd interrupted the moment?

But the shepherd wasn't nearby. He hadn't noticed she'd wandered off. He spun, searching the property. Destiny's barks grew louder, desperate. He spotted her bounding through the pasture, ducking beneath the split rail fence.

He looked farther and saw orange and yellow flames stretching into the sky, but the trees hindered his view of the point of origin.

Then an explosion rocked the ground.

EIGHT

Chance increased his pace, Ayla in stride with him, alternating cries for Marissa as they ran toward the fire.

Horses whinnied in terror from their pen near the flaming barn. Chance counted five. Where were the other three? They were far enough away that the flames hadn't yet reached them, but the danger had Lady, Arrow, Caesar and Dixie snorting and dragging their hooves along the soft ground. They ran the full length of the enclosure, kicking wildly and rearing up on their hind legs. Adjacent in a second, round corral, Tinkerbell paced, her head swaying from side to side.

"Where's Marissa?" Ayla hollered.

The flames were hot, crackling as the hungry fire consumed the wood and hay.

"Stay back!" Chance ordered. "Destiny and I will search for Marissa in the barn. Try to calm the horses and see if you can find the missing three." He feared they'd bolt and never be found.

"Okay."

"Destiny." The K-9 obediently jumped to his side, and he withdrew the short leash from his cargo pants, snapping it into place. "Seek."

Together they advanced toward the barn. Heat and

flames stretched to them from the rear, where the fire burned hottest. Shadow stood in his stall, the one closest to the entrance, whinnying and kicking wildly, his fear evident. Chance reached for the gate and swung it open. The horse was still haltered, so he grasped the lead and tugged him outside, transferring him to Ayla's care.

"Take Destiny also. It's too smoky in there."

She nodded, grasping the leash with one hand, the horse's harness with the other, and led the animals away.

Chance pulled his T-shirt up over his nose and mouth, then returned to the barn, searching for Marissa and the other two horses. He located Czar and Royal in their stalls at the farthest end of the building and, using their halters, led them out and passed them to Ayla.

Where was Marissa? Smoke consumed the interior, making it hard to see. Chance stayed low, surveying the stalls, and came up empty. He hurried to the far side and spotted boots and legs. The rest of her body was hidden behind a door. Chance entered and found Marissa unconscious in the tack room. Blackness covered the electronic control panel, and fire spurted from the box.

Marissa's right hand was badly burned. He touched her neck, feeling a pulse. *Thank You, Lord. Help me get her to safety.*

Chance lifted her limp body and ran out of the barn. Once they were a safe distance, he inhaled deeply, filling his lungs with fresh air and gently lowered her to the ground.

Ayla ran to his side, concern in her eyes.

"She's alive," he told her.

Ayla let out a shaky breath. "We have to get ropes and move the horses."

"I've got it. Call Walsh and request fire and rescue." He reached for his phone.

Ayla waved him off. "I have a phone. Go!"

Chance pulled the shirt over his nose and mouth again and rushed into the barn. The flames hungrily consumed the dry hay and straw on the stall floors and smoke burned his eyes as he searched for lead ropes, finally locating them hanging at the far side of the tack room. He hurried forward and snagged all of them, then turned and ran outside, unable to hold his breath any longer.

He gasped and coughed. Destiny sprinted to him, barking and anxiously pacing at his feet.

"Are you okay?" Ayla asked.

Chance nodded, still coughing, and passed Ayla a couple of the leads. "Can you start moving the horses?"

"Already in process, but I'll need help," Ayla replied. "I put Royal and Czar with Shadow in the corral at the far side of the pasture."

Wordlessly, Chance jogged beside her.

Ayla aimed for Lady and snapped a lead on her halter, then moved to Arrow. "Come on, sweetie. It's okay." Over her shoulder she said, "Whatever you do, stay calm. They feel your emotions."

"Stay with Marissa. I'll get the rest of the animals." Chance stepped into the ring, prepared to mimic her actions with Caesar and Dixie, but the two backed away from him, shaking their heads and snorting. His heart pounded, adrenaline coursing through his body. How was he supposed to stay calm? He exhaled, forcing his game face into place. *Calm. Must remain calm.*

"It's okay. Let's get you to the pen with your friends." He spoke slowly, inching closer to them and praying neither reared up and kicked him. Chance reached Dixie first and snapped the lead to her harness.

Then he turned toward Caesar, but the horse shifted.

"Come on, buddy. Please." Again, Chance stepped

forward, and the animal allowed him to attach the lead. "Good. We're halfway there." Unsure if he was doing it correctly, he opted to act confidently. Thankfully, the animals trailed him, and he forced himself to walk and not run to prevent frightening them. Thousands of pounds of horses stomping him in a panic did not sound fun.

He hurried down the lane to where Ayla stood at the eastern pasture. At his approach, she opened the gate, and together they ushered the animals inside.

Once he retrieved Tinkerbell and all eight horses were safely in the pen, he turned his attention to Marissa. Ayla knelt beside her, speaking softly.

"Where is the ambulance?" Impatience overrode his tone.

"Commander Walsh assured they were on their way along with the team."

But would they arrive in time? Chance squatted and checked Marissa's vitals again. Her shallow, labored breathing concerned him. "Please hold on," he whispered to her. "Help is coming."

Once more, he'd failed to spot trouble before it descended. The realization swarmed him. He'd depended on his abilities, his skills, and considered himself better than he was. He bowed his head and prayed, "Lord, I can't do this alone. Please help me. Save Marissa. God, we need You."

Minutes ticked by without a sign of rescue. Ayla prayed they'd make it in time to save Marissa. Crackling flames drew her attention. "Chance, we have to fight that fire before the whole place goes up in flames."

"Stay here. I'll go." Chance rose.

"No. We do this together."

They rushed to the barn. "Wait and let me see if I can find fire extinguishers."

She paused as he entered the barn, disappearing into the smoke. Ayla's anxiety ratcheted up, eager for his return. At last, he reappeared, carrying a red canister in each hand, and passed one to her.

"I turned off the circuit breaker for the barn, killing the electrical current. I think it started there. We must keep the fire from spreading to the house."

Ayla mimicked Chance's example and tugged her T-shirt over her mouth and nose as a barrier against the smoke.

They worked from the back of the barn forward, sweeping the foam across the stalls and floor until they'd exhausted both canisters.

Chance waved her outside, and they located a black hose. He turned the water on high, and they wet down the straw to prevent it from going up in flames. Though their efforts weren't useless, they struggled to tame the fire. Like a ravenous animal, it consumed everything in its path.

They reached the barn doors and heard the distant whine of sirens. Together they ran to check on Marissa. Destiny stood guard over her.

With one eye on Marissa and the other on the horses, Ayla marveled at how the animals didn't seem as distraught as they had earlier. They watched, fixated on her and Chance, as if to say, *take care of Marissa*. Ayla's eyes stung with tears. "We will," she promised.

Chance again checked Marissa's pulse.

Ayla's throat tightened, and her lungs hurt. "Lord, please help her." The sight of her new friend lying helpless in the grass made her heart ache.

This woman who had given so much to care for abused and mistreated animals lay unconscious with a severely burned hand. "Who would do such a thing?" Ayla looked up, meeting Chance's worried expression.

He worked his jaw, and anger flashed in his eyes. "Sutler."

"But why burn down the barn? Why not just shoot us?"

"He wanted to draw us out. We were down by the pond, away from the house, out of sight. I left Marissa an easy target."

"This is not on you!"

"It's my fault! You were both my responsibility." Chance succumbed to a coughing fit.

Unsure how to respond, Ayla shifted her focus to the real person at fault. "Sutler must've known something about Marissa. He didn't directly attack her or try to take her hostage."

"Agreed. With her military training, she'd have taken him out. He's a coward at every turn."

The sirens drew closer.

"Thank God Destiny warned us when she did. It could've been so much worse," Ayla said, stroking the shepherd who sat beside her, panting and reeking of smoke. "You did good, Destiny." The duo's teamwork continued to amaze her.

"Always trust your dog," Chance replied. "Ezra taught me that on day one." He reached up to stroke the dog's triangular ears. "You saved Marissa's life." He averted his gaze as though he feared speaking the words would somehow make them untrue.

"She's breathing," Ayla reassured him. But it was little comfort. "You think it was an electrical fire?"

"Yes. I saw dark marks around the control panel, and it explains Marissa's burned hand." He stood, reaching for his phone. "Where are the paramedics?"

Sirens blared louder in response. "They're close." Ayla spotted the strobing red lights rounding the bend.

A gasp for air got their full attention.

Chance fell to his knees beside Marissa and felt for a pulse. "No. No. No." He knelt over her and began CPR while Ayla stood helpless to assist. Why hadn't she learned to perform the lifesaving technique? She'd spent so much time protecting herself, she'd selfishly never considered she'd need to aid someone else.

Chance performed several chest compressions, then again checked her pulse. "Thank You, Lord, thank You, Lord," he prayed in an endless reel.

Ayla joined him, covering Marissa with their heartfelt pleas.

She glanced down, spotting the woman's rubber boots. "Her boots might've saved her from dying. Had she worn anything with metal in the boot—" Ayla didn't finish, and based on Chance's nod, he realized it, too.

At last, the emergency responder cavalry sped onto the property. The fire engine went straight to the barn while the ambulance screeched to a halt beside them and the paramedics jumped out. In a flurry of activity, they took over Marissa's care, and Ayla wrapped her arms around her torso.

They moved Marissa onto a stretcher, then loaded her into the back of the rig and sped from the property.

"Let's head to the house," Chance offered, gripping Destiny's leash. They'd started walking when his phone rang. "Commander."

Ayla listened as he spoke in clipped tones, sharing the details of the incident without emotion, but expressions of sadness and fury warred on his face.

"Yes, sir. Got it." He disconnected. "Walsh requested we load the horses into the trailer parked in the Morton building. He'll take them to the new location as soon as he gets here."

"Okay."

Chance jogged up the porch steps with Destiny beside him. He returned carrying keys and without his K-9. "I'll keep her in the house so she doesn't get in the way."

"That's smart. She'd want to help."

They rushed to where the firefighters worked to battle the barn blaze, which still raged despite Ayla and Chance's best efforts to extinguish it.

"The commander requested we move his horses into the trailer and prepare them for transport," Chance hollered to a man dressed in a white uniform shirt wearing a gold badge, indicating he was the fire chief.

"Go ahead. Steer clear of the rigs," he replied.

"Roger that."

Ayla followed Chance through the property to the enormous Morton building. They hurried to the large pickup truck, already attached to the horse trailer, and she climbed into the passenger seat. They rumbled out of the building and down the lane, carefully bypassing the firefighters by driving on the edge of the gravel road. Ayla winced at the damage the tires would do to the grounds. But it couldn't be helped. They had to load the animals.

When they reached the eastern pen, they exited the truck.

"Calm," Ayla reminded Chance as much as herself.

"Right." Chance lowered the massive rear door, exposing the individual places for each horse. Then, snagging the lead ropes from where they'd left them on the rails of the corral, they each approached the closest horse.

"One at a time," Chance said.

Ayla moved to Shadow. "Hey, sweetie." She gently took his halter and snapped on the lead rope, then led him through the gate and up the trailer ramp. She placed him in the farthest stall. "Thank you for being compliant."

Chance entered with Arrow. He spoke softly, reassuring the animal.

Ayla hurried out and secured Dixie while Chance got Lady. She was not pleased with the arrangement. "I know you're scared," he said. "I promise we'll do everything we can to help."

Ayla blinked away tears as she exited the trailer and aimed for Caesar. The horse's dark eyes met hers with a tenderness that nearly undid her. "She's going to make it," she assured the horse. "Please, Lord, let Marissa be okay."

When they'd finished loading the remaining horses, Chance closed the large door.

His phone rang, and he answered on speakerphone. "Commander."

"ETA twenty. What's the update?" Walsh's voice, though controlled, held a slight quiver.

"EMTs took Marissa to Mercy First Hospital. According to them, she's in critical condition."

"I'll head there. The team is on their way to you. I'll catch up after I've spoken to the doctors."

"Understood."

"But you'll have to drive the horses to the location I texted to you."

"Got it, not a problem," Chance replied.

"Good. Thank you."

"I'm so sorry," Ayla said, the words inadequate to convey her apology.

"This isn't on you, Ayla," Walsh replied.

"We'll take care of the animals, sir. We're at the far eastern pasture, so we'll head back and get an update from the fire chief."

"Just text it to me. I need to check on Marissa." Pain

tightened the man's voice and Ayla wanted to say something to comfort him, but words failed her.

"Roger that," Chance replied, and they disconnected.

As they headed back, Ayla stumbled, and Chance caught her in his arms. He placed a hand on the small of her back, bracing her. "Why is this happening?" she asked him.

"We have a crafty enemy. But we're going to take Sutler and his men down."

"You can't promise that. No one can." Ayla's eyes welled with tears. "How many innocent people will die because of me?"

Chance stopped and forced her to face him. "Walsh said it and I'll say it again. None of this is your fault. You didn't cause this. Don't give up. We're going to win this battle."

Ayla looked down, a tear streaking her cheek. "But at what cost?"

He pulled her close, and she didn't resist. Instead, she absorbed his strength. As she turned her head to rest it against his chest, she saw the firefighters and police officers swarming the property. "Lord, help them."

Maybe she needed to go. The longer she stayed, no matter where, she inflicted danger on those around her. A whinny from inside the trailer jolted her to the present. Ayla swiped at her cheek. The horses could've been killed, too. Her resolve set, she determined once they knew Marissa would survive, she'd leave. She'd find a way to disappear.

Chance stepped back. "I'll go talk with the fire chief and let him know the team's on their way, and we'll return as soon as we take care of the horses."

"Okay."

He glanced at the trailer. "I don't want to move this. Would you mind retrieving Destiny? Then meet me back here?"

"Not a problem," Ayla replied.

They headed up the lane where rescue crews had spread out, working to keep the flames from reaching the house.

"I don't want to get in everyone's way."

"Maybe go through the back door with Destiny?" Chance suggested.

"Good idea."

They parted ways through the chaos. Chance aimed for the chief, who was barking orders into a radio, and Ayla sidestepped several firefighters dragging hoses. She spotted Destiny perched in the window and made her way around the back of the house. The shepherd's sharp barks urged Ayla to hurry and release her.

"Ma'am?"

She turned.

A firefighter dressed in bunker gear approached. His helmet shadowed his face. "Ma'am, I'm supposed to ask you to come with me. Chief's orders."

Ayla shielded her eyes from the sun, unable to see him clearly.

"Sorry," the firefighter said. "It's so chaotic down there."

"Sure. Where?"

"Something to do with a horse trailer?"

Ayla's pulse ratcheted. "What's wrong?"

"I'm not sure. Chief just said one of them was hurt or had gotten out or something. He was yelling so fast I couldn't catch everything. Anyway, your friend Chance asked if you could help. He said to hold off getting his dog."

Ayla glanced up at Destiny, barking and pawing at the window. Taking the animal down to the horses might upset them. "Um, okay." She spun on her heel.

"Thanks a lot. I'm new on the department. Gotta show the chief I can follow orders and all that."

"Uh-huh." What had happened in the short time she

and Chance had parted? Had one of the horses escaped the trailer?

"This is a shortcut. It'll keep us out of the way of them working the fire." She led him to the side, hidden from the firefighters.

"I'd hoped you say that."

She turned around at the strange words just as a strike to her neck dropped Ayla to the ground. "What—"

"Time to go, Ayla," he said. "You've been a real nuisance."

Confusion and terror swarmed her. Through blurred vision, she blinked. The man stood over her. She tried to turn her head to scream, but nothing came out. He put a hand over her mouth, and a sting in her arm sent the world spinning before everything went black.

Chance waited to talk to the chief. The chaos had the man torn in a hundred directions. Finally, he made his way through and explained the situation.

He aimed for the trailer. Barking and thudding caught his attention, and he turned to the house. Destiny barked and clawed at the front window. She hated being away from the action, but she'd never acted so erratically before.

Where was Ayla? He scanned the property. Was she inside? Or had she given up after his dog went wild?

He shifted direction and headed toward the house. Destiny's barks grew louder, more desperate, and she threw herself against the glass. Chance's instincts blared on high alert, and he accidentally bumped into a firefighter working to extinguish flames that had jumped to the long grass. "Sorry."

The man gave him a dismissive nod.

Chance hurried up the hill to the house, pushing past the rescue workers without comment. He bolted up the porch steps and through the door. Destiny plowed into him. She barked and raged, barely giving him time to snap on her leash. "What's wrong? Ayla!"

No answer.

His eyes roved the space.

The lack of response told him everything he needed and didn't want to know. She was gone. "No. No. Ayla!"

Destiny bolted outside, straining against her leash.

He ran with her and paused by the rescue workers closest to the house. "Have you seen Ayla? The woman with me?"

The first rescue worker shook his head. "Sorry, man, focused on the fire."

Chance ran to the next with the same inquiry. He continued asking everyone, but they hadn't seen her. She couldn't have just disappeared. Destiny pulled toward the tree line, and he knew it was up to them to find her. They rushed to the house and Chance grabbed Ayla's nightshirt, holding it out for Destiny. "Seek." The dog sniffed at the fabric and Chance repeated the order. "Destiny! Seek!"

The shepherd lunged for the side of the house, taking the shortcut, and nearly yanked his arm from its socket. Chance spotted a syringe in the grass and held back Destiny. Using his sleeve, he picked it up. A drop of clear liquid remained in the vial. He set it next to the house.

As he straightened up, he noticed the window above looked right down on them. Destiny had seen what had happened to Ayla, which explained her uncharacteristic behavior.

"Destiny. Seek!"

She took him through the trees, zigzagging through the low-hanging branches and thick evergreens. Chance ducked and swiped at the greenery scraping his face, all the while praying. He had to find her. "Ayla!"

They crested the hill and Destiny continued pulling him. Ayla couldn't have gotten far.

At last, they reached a dirt path carved with tire marks. The old, worn road had deep potholes, confirming it hadn't been used in a long time.

Destiny stopped and whined.

Whoever had taken Ayla had driven to this location. Chance removed his cell phone from his pocket, intending to use the mapping features, then realized all he had was the burner phone. With a sigh, he made the call he dreaded. Though he didn't want to bother Commander Walsh, he had to update him on the situation.

"What's wrong?" Walsh answered on the first ring.

Chance sucked in a breath and said, "Someone took Ayla." He provided the sliver of information he knew.

"He stalked you!" Walsh growled. "I'll notify the team. I'm almost to the hospital. Once I've spoken to the doctors, I'll head your way."

"Sir, I want to continue the search, but Destiny lost the scent at the dirt road. And I'm not even sure where it goes."

"Where are you?"

Chance turned, surveying the area, and provided the best coordinates and landmarks possible.

"Okay, I think you're near the old minimum maintenance road. It's not used anymore and very rough. However, it leads to the highway. There are too many options for which direction they'd go."

Chance ran a hand through his hair, desperation and frustration mingling. "I don't know where to start."

"Return to the house. We have security cameras. I'll give Tiandra the information she needs to pull the footage. I'll be there soon." Walsh disconnected without another word.

"Destiny, why didn't I keep you with me?" Chance

stared up at the cloudless sky. "Lord, I don't deserve to ask for anything from You. I've certainly not been the best about keeping in touch and praying daily. I'm trying to do better, but God, Ayla needs You. Please, somehow give us what we need to find her."

The walk to the house was the longest one Chance had ever taken. He received a text advising him the team had arrived. When he rounded Walsh's house, he spotted the familiar SUVs.

Graham jogged to him. "Walsh updated us. I'll take the trailer to the location he wants. You and Tiandra work on the footage."

Unable to speak, he stood silent. He'd failed in every way possible. As a team member, as Ayla's handler and as her protector. What could he possibly say? There was no excuse for his ineptitude. He looked at the remaining rescue personnel as they concluded their roles to quench the fire. In the chaos and the multitude of people there, how had he not noticed someone lurking about?

"Blaming yourself won't help anything," Tiandra said.

Chance looked up, not realizing she'd approached. "How can I not? I messed up. So bad."

"Sutler is brilliant in a horrible, criminal sort of way. We were sure this would be a safe place for you. And we were wrong."

Chance shook his head. "It's all on me."

Graham exited the property, driving the Ford pickup with the horse trailer in tow.

"We'll find her," Tiandra assured him. "But we won't do that standing here debating who should suffer most for this. We can fight about that later."

Chance nodded and walked with her. Bosco and Destiny moved in step with them as though they understood the seriousness of the situation. Skyler and Riker, with

Ammo beside him, worked with the fire chief, no doubt
going over the same things Chance had in search of Ayla.

They entered the house, and Tiandra headed for the
basement. Confused, Chance followed her, the dogs with
him. They stopped in the living room, and she rounded
the counter. He stepped closer, and she pressed a button
and a larger panel opened in the wall, revealing a key-
board and a laptop.

As the canines sat beside the couch, Chance hovered
over Tiandra, unable to sit.

Tiandra typed, bringing the movie screen to life, revealing panels with ten camera views. She continued typing,
and the footage changed.

"I'm reversing one hour to see if we can find the perp
first. Then we'll see who set the fire."

Chance's gaze remained transfixed on the screen, and
he rushed forward. "There!"

A man dressed in bunker gear emerged through the tree
line where Chance and Destiny had gone in search of Ayla.

"That's how he moved around here unnoticed."

"Yep," Tiandra replied. "And I'm guessing he had that
all ready to go before he started the fire. He just needed
the crews to show up." She scrolled to one of the cameras.

On the screen Ayla spoke to the firefighter before
rounding the house. Tiandra shifted to a different location, spotting the man as he struck Ayla on the neck. She
fell, clearly stunned. Then he injected her arm, and she
flopped limp into the grass.

"I found that syringe. He dropped it on the ground."
Chance rushed from the room and returned with it in his
sleeved hand. He snagged an evidence bag from the kit
sitting on the table and passed it to Tiandra.

"Good," she said, surveying the bag. "Maybe we'll get
fingerprints off it."

Like voyeurs to the crime, they continued to watch as the man lifted Ayla and walked to the west into the tree line.

"Yes!" Tiandra said.

Chance spun on his heel to face her. "What?"

"Walsh thought the perp might go that way. He has wildlife cameras out there." Tiandra changed screens, revealing a sepia-colored video.

On the screen Destiny and Chance walked to the site where the K-9 lost the scent. In a continued reversal, Tiandra brought up the footage of the man loading Ayla into the back of an SUV.

"Can we get the plate?" Hope rose in Chance's heart.

"We're going to do our best," Tiandra said, typing. She connected a cord to the laptop, and using her phone, swiped at the screen. "Downloading to our server," she explained. "The make and model are common. I'll work on it from our computers and see if I can sort through the pixelated footage."

"It's pretty bad."

"I've seen worse." Tiandra called in an APB for the vehicle.

"Do you think the all-points bulletin will work?"

"We're going to do everything possible." Tiandra typed a text into her phone. "We'll get this data to Eliana Kastell. She'll keep digging while we pray and sift whatever clues we find." She referenced Riker's wife and the team's technical expert.

"You do that? I mean, pray, even when you don't have to in the team meetings?"

They'd met at the Rock, the nickname for the Heartland Fugitive Task Force headquarters. Chance had participated by closing his eyes, but he'd never spoken aloud and secretly feared they'd force him. To him, faith was private, not something talked about with coworkers.

"We don't do it because we *have* to," Tiandra, said smiling. "Our faith is our foundation, and without God working through us and our cases, we're hopeless to solve anything. There's power in prayer."

"I pray," Chance said defensively, hating that he'd broached the topic.

"I'm not judging you."

The comment floored him. No, he was the one judging. "I'm sorry."

"Don't be. We're all learning and growing in our faith. The team has taught me a lot over the years. Not just in tactical operations, but developing my spiritual skills, too."

"I need that."

"No pressure. Be you."

Chance grimaced. If only he knew what that meant. "I'd like to get to the point of praying with you guys, but it's uncomfortable for me."

"That's okay. Prayer is between you and God. Don't feel obligated to join us. That's useless. I talk to God just as you and I are talking. One on one, normal verbiage and honest."

"I'm used to praying for big stuff only."

"It took me a while to get over my vending machine prayers."

Chance grinned. "What?"

"You know, 'God, gimme this to make me happy,' like you're inserting money into a vending machine. Then end with 'amen,' like pushing the button and taking a candy bar."

"Ouch."

"Sounds familiar?"

"A little."

"God wants a relationship with you. More than gimme this or that. It's a way of transforming your thinking. He's in control and sovereign. Even when we don't understand, we trust Him. That's prayer."

Chance nodded. His grandpa had said the same things, but somewhere along the line, Chance had forgotten. "Thanks, Tiandra."

"Anytime." She returned to the laptop.

Chance bowed his head. *Lord, I'm sorry for treating You like a vending machine. I want a real relationship with You. I know You'll turn this for good somehow, but I'm scared and worried. Help me to release this into Your hands. Protect Ayla. Please.*

Heavy footfalls preceded Skyler and Riker, along with Ammo, bounding down the stairs to join them. "Graham's on his way back. Horses are safe and secure."

"Awesome," Tiandra said.

"Hey, let's huddle and pray. We've got a lot to deal with," Riker said.

The group rallied in the center of the room, and Riker began the prayer. Chance's heart felt as if it would beat out of his chest. Would they expect him to talk? What was he supposed to say? He started practicing his part in his mind. But the collective "Amen" happened before he could say anything.

He opened his eyes. The team stared at him.

"You all right, bro?" Riker quirked a brow. "Did we stop you from praying?"

"No. I, uh…" Chance stammered.

"He's just major stressed about finding Ayla." Tiandra jumped to his defense.

He shot her a grateful nod.

"We'll find her." Riker smacked him on the back.

"Let's delve deeper into the footage." Tiandra typed in more information, and the cameras reversed to several hours prior. A man, similar in build as Ayla's kidnapper and wearing a baseball cap that shielded his face, stood shadowed near the barn, watching Marissa in the pasture. Zink strolled beside him.

"That's gotta be him," Chance said.

The man attempted to kick Zink and missed. The cat hissed, hopped onto the fence and swiped, clawing his face. He jerked back. Zink bolted through the pasture before the man finished swinging his fist.

As if on cue, a meow preceded the orange tabby, who appeared on the steps and trotted down.

"Dude, you got a great swipe in." Chance hoisted the feline into his arms. He glanced up, catching Riker's amused grin.

Skyler and Tiandra chuckled. "I never pictured you as a cat man."

"Zink here might've gotten some helpful crime-solving DNA in his claws," Chance said. "And we'll identify the guy by Zink's claw marks."

"That might be a long shot, but I'm willing to try." Skyler gently took Zink into her arms. "Let's do a little kitty swab on those brilliant weapons of yours and see what we can find." She carried the cat upstairs, cooing and stroking his orange fur.

Chance returned to watching the screen.

Marissa rode Shadow in the pasture, carefree and smiling, completely unaware of her upcoming fate. The idea sickened Chance. His gaze roved the scene, returning to the man lingering in the shadows. "Pause that, please."

Tiandra did as he asked.

"He's wearing a black backpack, and I don't see a gun. Isn't that strange?"

"Not if he knew exactly what he was here for. If he'd wanted to assassinate you all, he would've. He needs Ayla alive to find the list." She played the video.

The man entered the barn, returning shortly afterward,

completely undetected by any of them. He still wore the backpack, though it appeared less bulky as he strolled through the tree line. His demeanor was carefree, as if he had all the time in the world. Chance's shoulders tensed and his hands were tightly fisted at his sides as he watched the man disappear.

"They sent him in to destroy the barn—to set the fire as a distraction," Riker said.

"Marissa was collateral damage," Tiandra said. "If they weren't sure y'all were here, it gave them a way to draw you out."

"Exactly," Graham said, joining the team.

"But now that they have Ayla, what will they do?" Riker asked.

Tiandra looked down, and Skyler remained quiet.

A rock seemed to lodge in Chance's throat. They'd do whatever they had to do to extract the information from Ayla.

And then kill her.

NINE

Jerked from peaceful rest, Ayla attempted, unsuccessfully, to open her eyes. She drifted off again until the harsh ringing of a phone, followed by a man's voice, dragged her from the comfortable lure of sleep. As her eyes opened, she realized she was in the back of a vehicle, her hands bound. She gasped, inhaling glue from the tape covering her mouth. Panic threatened to consume her, and she struggled to remain calm. Her pulse raged so hard in her ears, she feared they'd explode.

"Yeah, she's still out," the man said. "What a lightweight."

She recognized his voice as the impostor firefighter who'd kidnapped her. Ayla stilled to listen.

He paused before snapping, "Why are we keeping her alive, then?"

Ayla blinked. At least she wouldn't die immediately. That was a plus.

"Ha, sure." His creepy cackle sent a shiver through her.

She winced against the drug coursing through her body. Nausea and a throbbing headache did a nasty tango. Whatever he'd injected her with wasn't leaving her system without a fight.

"Should be there in an hour." Silence. "Made a couple stops on the way. Got it."

Ayla prepared to die.

While her mind volleyed with her last moments on earth, her heart returned to Chance. A twinge of hope that he'd find her gave Ayla the desire to live.

But what if she never saw him again? Why hadn't she told him how she felt? Images of the marshal's chiseled features and solid muscular frame warmed her. Ayla's mind drifted to Chance's gentle ways with Destiny. Combined with his take-charge personality, he checked off every box required for the perfect guy. Funny, sweet and thoughtful. He had it all. And for the first time, she realized being with Chance had awakened her heart to the possibility of love.

Too bad she'd never experience it.

He'd never know that she'd fallen for him.

The vehicle stopped abruptly, and she rolled into the back seat, jerking her to the present.

Her kidnapper had enjoyed driving fast and slamming on the brakes as a game to hurt her.

"Oh, yeah, I'll get the information out of her." His comment to the unknown party on the phone sucked the air from her lungs.

What did that mean? She closed her eyes and listened.

Though he couldn't see her from the driver's seat, she figured it benefited her more for him to think she was unconscious.

Again, the vehicle lurched forward, and Ayla rolled backward with the force. The tape across her mouth made it hard to breathe. Self-talk to remain calm was the only thing that prevented her from hyperventilating. She lay on her side, her cheek pressed against the rough vehicle carpet.

The driver guffawed. "No promises, but I won't kill her."

He flipped on the radio, and the speakers vibrated with the blaring country music. Her captor sang along out of tune.

Ayla shifted from her prone position, discovering he'd left her ankles free. *Loser.* He should've taken extra effort to ensure she didn't escape.

She took in her surroundings. From the rounded sides and windows of the vehicle, it was not a car or truck. Possibly an SUV, since the back seat blocked her view of the driver. The acrid scent of smoke on her clothing hung in the air, adding to her queasy stomach. Flickers of sunlight faded into twilight.

Ayla lifted her hands, inspecting the binding. She wiggled her fingers to awaken the digits with blood flow and rid her hands of the pins-and-needles sensation. How long had she been out? Had they driven the entire time? Where was he taking her?

The questions roiled, breeding anxiety. *God, I'm scared. What do I do?*

She pictured Ezra, speaking in his strict instructor tone. *Disorientation and confusion are the enemy's weapons. God is not the author of confusion. He's given you clarity and peace. Silence the enemy by leaning into Him.*

Ayla gave her best effort to inhale through her nose, calming her mind with prayer. *Lord, You're not surprised by these events. Show me the way.*

Step one, free her wrists.

She lifted her hands, realizing she'd skipped ahead. First, she'd have to rip the tape off her mouth.

Ayla used her fingernails to pick at the adhesive. She released a tiny corner. *Yes!* The tires dipped into a hole, throwing her off balance.

She righted herself and continued working at the tape until she peeled a section free. Again, the vehicle jolted her, and she rolled sideways. An object pressed against her hip bone.

The cheap cell phone Marissa had given to her!

Her kidnapper had missed the small device hidden in her jeans pocket.

Ayla shifted slightly, lifting her hip, and, using the heels of her bound hands, scooted the phone free. She extracted it with her fingers. But how would she dial?

She rolled to her other side, facing the back seat, and placed the cell down, laying her ear on it. She couldn't talk with the man listening. And she'd have to silence the buttons and ringtone first. Unfamiliar with the phone's mechanics and using only the heels of her hands and fingertips, she worked to locate the volume, then with her short fingernails, she dialed 9-1-1. She pressed her cheek against the device to muffle the sound and prayed he didn't hear.

Ringing.

Answer! She willed the dispatcher on the other end of the line to comply with her demands.

A second ring.

At last, the dispatcher answered, "9-1-1, what's your emergency?"

Keeping her voice a mere whisper, Ayla said, "Help! My name is Ayla DuPree. I've been kidnapped."

"Ma'am, I can't hear you."

The driver continued screeching along with the radio from the front seat.

"I can't talk louder. Help me. I'm in an SUV. Contact Chance Tavalla at the Heartland Fugitive Task Force."

"Ma'am, slow down. Where are you?"

"Listen! He's going to kill me! Trace this call. I don't know where I am, but send help. Please tell Deputy US Marshal Chance Tavalla!"

The radio shut off. "Well, look who is finally awake," the man said.

Was he aware she'd called 9-1-1? He was either stupid

or had forgotten he'd gagged her. Regardless, she needed to get information to the dispatcher. "Where are you taking me?" She spoke loudly, praying the dispatcher overheard his response.

"Ma'am, who are you talking to?" the dispatcher asked.

"You abducted me from the Walsh horse rescue in Ponca. Where are you taking me?" Ayla replied, giving the dispatcher any details she could. "You pretended to be a firefighter."

"Yeah, worked perfectly, too." He chuckled. "Don't you worry, darlin'. Sutler's got plans for you."

"Myles Sutler with the EastSide7 gang is waiting for me? Does he know I was in witness protection?"

"Why are you asking so many questions?"

The road grew rough, and Ayla fought to maintain her hold on the phone. He hit a bump, and her cheek bounced against the phone, depressing a button.

She froze in place. Had he heard the sound?

"Can you see any signs or landmarks?" the dispatcher asked.

Ayla didn't respond. Her kidnapper was listening.

"Ma'am, are you still there?"

"Where are you taking me?" she repeated.

"Hey, how're you talking?" Great, the lightbulb over his dim brain finally illuminated and he'd remembered he'd gagged her. The man slammed on the brakes, and Ayla's face scraped against the hard automotive carpeting. The phone started to slide away.

She pressed her cheek down harder, fighting not to lose the device. "Help! Help me!"

The driver's door opened, casting light inside the SUV.

"He's coming!" Panic tightened Ayla's chest. "Please help me!"

Heavy footsteps drew closer.

"Ma'am, I'm trying to help you. Stay on the line with me."

"Hurry! Please hurry! I'm in an SUV. Call Marshal Tavalla! Please!"

The hatch door swung upward, and the sound of cicadas filled the air.

"Help!" Ayla cried again. She peered over her shoulder. The man hovered inches from her face. His breath smelled of alcohol and nicotine.

In slow motion, the scene unraveled before her. For the first time, she saw her kidnapper. A large scratch stretched from his forehead to his crooked nose. His cavernous dark eyes and murderous glower lingered on her. Then his lips cracked into a snarling smile. "Aren't you a sneaky hag?"

"What's your location?" the dispatcher asked.

He shifted his gaze and looked to the phone hidden beside her. His eyes narrowed, and he reached over her, yanking out a handful of Ayla's hair with the phone.

In one last desperate plea, Ayla yelled, "Help!"

The man reared back and punched her, silencing her cry. Pain mingled with shock, and the taste of copper filled her mouth. He looked at the phone as though seeing it for the first time. Perhaps contemplating the implications of his lack of judgment in not searching Ayla.

The dispatcher's voice carried to her, "Ma'am. Ma'am. Are you there?"

"Sorry, wrong number," he said, tossing the phone to the ground with a soft thud. He stomped his foot and shattered the device.

Ayla spun on her back, thrusting her feet at his chest.

He stumbled backward, and she scooted out of the SUV. Her boots touched the gravel, and she bolted in an awkward sprint before she regained her balance. Ayla ran with all her strength into the field.

Tall grass whipped at her legs as she frantically surveyed the acres of cornfields and pastures for shelter or help.

Crickets chirruped in their night songs, cheering her on to safety.

Was the man behind her? With her wrists still bound, Ayla struggled to keep her momentum. Her lungs burned as she pushed harder, determined to gain as much distance as possible.

Would the dispatcher find her location? Would help come in time?

Her feet slammed hard on the uneven earth, and in her peripheral she caught sight of the man chasing her.

A gunshot exploded the night air.

She dodged left and circled a massive bale of prairie grass. Several more shots sprayed pieces like confetti around her.

Ayla took off again. The open pasture offered no shelter.

The man was fast, but he stopped several times to shoot, giving Ayla the opportunity to create more distance.

The sun had set, plunging them into darkness and making the trek more difficult. It also provided shadows for Ayla. At the end of the pasture, she noticed a creek bed in the valley bordered by trees. Ayla increased her speed, aiming for the foliage. Her chest stung with exertion as she ducked into the downed branches and peered out.

The man stood, gun trained in the direction she'd run, but his posture indicated he'd lost her. Ayla crept through the tree line. She couldn't stay in the valley and going uphill might reveal her location. Still, she had to keep moving.

She left the security of the trees and crested a large hill, exhaling relief when she saw the house in the distance.

Lord, give me strength. Ayla infused every last blast of

energy she could muster into her legs. Glancing over her shoulder, she saw the man running toward her.

No. She'd come so far.

A five-foot wire mesh fence surrounded the property. Too high to jump. The fence wobbled slightly as she braced her hands on it, pulling herself over. The wires swayed, and she tumbled off into a thistle patch. Ayla got to her feet, her hands stinging from the thorns still imbedded in her flesh.

Can't stop.

She hollered for help, praying someone inside the house would come out. But the lights were off, and it appeared deserted. Only a few feet more to go.

Ayla stumbled, her legs shaking.

A tackle from behind flattened her on the rocky earth.

She screamed and squirmed, trying to free herself of the man's constricting hold.

He pressed his knee into her kidneys, inflicting pain. He held his position, allowing Ayla to writhe. "That was foolish! And you've cost us time!"

"I'm sorry, I'm sorry," she pleaded, desperate for him to move off her.

He shifted to the side, and she gasped for air.

But he wasn't through.

His strong hand flexed into her hair, grabbing at the roots, and he lifted her off the ground. She yelped, staggering to her feet.

He stood, inches from her face. Even in the dim light, Ayla saw the vicious glower on his face. He panted, chest heaving, and pressed the gun against her temple. "If Sutler didn't need you alive, I'd kill you."

She shook with adrenaline and fear, unable to form words in response.

Still holding her hair, he turned, as though surveying

the property. "You'll experience Sutler's fury when I tell him about your call."

He dragged her to the side of the house where double hatch doors slanted into the grassy hillside. An outdoor cellar.

Then the man shoved Ayla to the ground and drove his knee into her chin.

The hit forced her to bite her tongue, and stars danced in front of her eyes. She curled on her side, protecting her vital organs.

"Oh, no. You're going to pay." He jerked her up, twisting her arm so tight Ayla feared he'd snap the bone. He tugged open one of the cellar doors.

Ayla reared back, trying to steer clear of the cavernous pit he'd revealed.

He pressed his face against hers, scratching her skin with his prickly facial hair. "What's wrong? Afraid of the dark?"

Terror squeezed her chest like a vise.

Ayla thrust her leg into his knee, causing it to hyperextend. He yowled and she took off, running toward the front of the house. Surely there was a road. Someone would see her.

The man's curses trailed her, but she didn't turn to see where he was.

She felt the sting before she heard the gunshot and dropped to the ground. Her calf burned with the intensity of a thousand torches.

Then he was on her. In one swift movement, he rolled her onto her back. Ayla sucked in a breath just as his fist pummeled her face.

Pain exploded through her nose, and her eyes watered, blurring her vision.

Several more punches resulted in an iron-and-copper taste filling her mouth.

He called her vile names, screaming and cursing her, but the hits caused her ears to ring with such intensity, she barely heard him.

The man yanked her to her feet, but Ayla's leg refused to bear her weight. "I can't walk," she pleaded.

A stony grin stretched across his face, and he guffawed. "Well, good. You won't be running away this time, will you?"

She tried shifting from one foot to the other, wincing with the pain.

"You know the best part of this? You're so stupid that you ran right to the place I wanted you." He tsked and chortled. "I'll give you the knee strike, though. Well done."

Her eyes drilled into his. *I'm not afraid of you.* Ezra's instructions played in her mind. *Let your will to live override your fear. You can't afford fear's drain on your energy.*

The kidnapper chuckled. "Ezra taught you well. Too bad his training didn't save him."

At the words, tears threatened. No, she wouldn't grieve for Ezra right now.

"Try another stunt, and I'll make sure it's your last. Sutler wants you alive, but that doesn't stop me from inflicting agony. Got me?"

She glowered at him, fury at the man's horrid threats rising within her.

"That's a scary face." He guffawed. "Save it for Sutler." He slapped her upside the head, then hoisted her over his shoulders in a fireman's carry. The irony wasn't lost on her. The guy had been a wannabe firefighter.

Bile rose in her throat, worsening at every bounce against his shoulder. She surveyed the house as they approached, gathering as many details as possible for her escape. The old clapboard farmhouse, circa 1930s, clearly neglected based on the lack of care. A single bulb flickered from the front porch, casting eerie light. Mature trees lined the grounds on the south side like guardians, concealing them from the road.

He carried her back to the cellar, then set her down on the ground.

"So." He squatted before her, his dark eyes burrowing into hers.

Ayla fought the urge to headbutt him.

"This is how it's going to go. Sutler's on his way. He's not nearly as nice as I am, so you'd better take advantage of my kindness. Tell me where RJ Warden hid the list. If you lie to me, I'll hurt you." He raised his fist, emphasizing the comment.

She flinched, the memory of his attack still fresh in her mind.

"I don't know. After everything I've endured, don't you think I'd hand it over? That list means nothing to me. It's certainly not worth dying over." Her words came out rapid fire, but she was desperate.

He shook his head. "See, now I thought you'd be smarter than that."

"I'm telling you the truth!"

"No, you're not. Guess I'll let Sutler handle you." He made a show of tsking and wagging his finger in her face. "Too bad. He's got harsher methods of getting people to talk." He hoisted her up over his shoulder again.

"No, please, no!" She pounded his back with her still bound fists.

He stood over the darkened hole. "Tuck and roll." He laughed and tossed her inside.

Chance paced the living room in the Walshes' basement, tackled from every direction by memories of Ayla.

Her beautiful smile and delightful laughter. The way one side of her full lips quirked when she questioned him. Her emerald gaze that had penetrated his heart, prompting him to reveal things about himself he'd avoided admitting. And the truth of his feelings for her, despite everything that kept her off-limits.

Ayla consumed him, and the worry of dangers she faced alone, in the hands of a dangerous and lethal criminal, threatened to steal Chance's composure.

The team sat in the basement, now converted to their base of operations. Over the past twenty-four hours, they contemplated scenarios, made endless calls and debated their next steps. They'd also sifted through the video, pulling every possible clue from the footage, and still came up empty.

Walsh's cameras didn't show the place where Chance and Ayla had shared the briefest kiss, but he'd confessed the truth of his botches in detail to them. None of the HFTF group had spoken a condemning word. Riker had met his wife, Eliana, while providing her protective detail, so they had firsthand experience of how the heart had its own agenda. Subsequently, Eliana had joined HFTF as the technical expert.

He half-heartedly listened, unable to focus past his unending prayers. "Lord, help us," he said under his breath. In his peripheral, he caught Skyler's compassionate expression.

"The fire marshal confirms Marissa sustained injuries from electrocution, thanks to whoever provided that *creative*—" Walsh spat the word with venom "—little setup in the tack room." His rigid posture and the stiff line of his jaw showed the indignation they all shared at Marissa's attack. "Looks like the criminal cut the power, baiting her to look there, and when she touched the panel, she was electrocuted. The subsequent blast was a result of a timed bomb rigged to explode as a secondary detonation."

"Conceivably, the bomber assumed the first event would draw in Ayla, allowing him to kidnap her, then finish Chance and Marissa with the explosion," Skyler said.

Chance winced. Had he done his job, instead of strolling the property with Ayla, he'd have noticed the bomber. Yet, the sweet moment with her was something he'd not trade, especially since it fueled him past hopelessness. The internal battle warred on, chastening him with *should've, could've, would've* scenarios while his heart clung to the awakening Ayla brought to him.

No. He'd failed. Protecting Ayla and Marissa was his sole duty. He should've stopped the whole thing before Marissa got hurt. And based on Walsh's stony stare, he concurred. Condemnation cloaked Chance with an overwhelming weight.

"Agreed," Walsh said.

"Sutler's convinced Ayla has the list," Graham said.

Reengaging himself with the discussion, Chance replied, "His unwillingness to accept anything else might be what keeps Ayla alive."

"Or the catalyst for him to hurt her," Riker added.

Chance shot him a glare. "Thanks for that." He groaned and resumed pacing.

"Dude." Graham chastised Riker with a glower.

Riker winced. "Sorry."

"The statement is accurate." Walsh's phone rang, and he excused himself.

"Don't say it, Graham. I know," Riker said. "I need to work on my delivery method."

"Yeah, maybe toss the words around in your head before you blurt them," Graham replied.

"Cut him some slack. We're not used to tragedies hitting so close to our own," Tiandra defended.

Walsh returned, cutting the discussion short. "We have a lead." The group stilled as Walsh relayed the information. "Ayla made a 9-1-1 call."

"What? How?" Chance blurted.

Skyler tapped away at her laptop. "Listen." She played the recording, and the breath left Chance's lungs at the desperation and fear in Ayla's voice.

"Contact Chance Tavalla at the Heartland Fugitive Task Force."

"Ma'am, slow down. Where are you?"

"Listen! He's going to kill me! Trace this call. I don't know where I am, but send help. Please tell Deputy US Marshal Chance Tavalla!"

Chance moved closer to the laptop listening as Ayla spoke. "She's trying to give the dispatcher information to find her." Brilliant. The woman was facing a killer and still she had the wherewithal to think clearly.

Ayla. *Oh, God, please show us where she is.*

Unable to breathe at the panic in Ayla's tone, Chance clung to the countertop. Though he wanted to run from the room, he required every detail from the call.

"What's your location?" the dispatcher asked.

"Help!"

The muffled cries from Ayla tore at Chance. She'd needed him and he hadn't been there. She'd called his name, and more than anything he wanted to respond. Then finally he heard, "Sorry, wrong number," followed by a thud, and the line went dead. Chance fisted his hands to keep from punching the closest person.

He met Tiandra's worried expression, but to her credit, she didn't say anything.

Chance stared at the laptop as though doing so would produce Ayla.

"That's all." Skyler stepped closer, placing a hand on his shoulder, but he shrugged it off.

He didn't deserve comfort. He averted his eyes and turned to stare out the window to the empty pasture where Walsh's rescue horses and his kind sister should've occupied the beautiful landscape. Instead, Marissa lay unconscious in the hospital, fighting for her life, and Ayla was in the clutches of an EastSide7 kidnapper.

"The dispatcher tracked the cell phone for most of the short connection. Since the account belongs to Walsh, we have authorization from the cellular company to triangulate the call," Tiandra said. "I've got a search area established that should put us within five miles of the tower. However, since the trace started late, and the call ended shortly thereafter, we have a delayed tracking start point."

"What're we waiting for?" Chance moved to the door, and Destiny joined him.

With a few more swipes and taps on her computer, Tiandra sent the detailed map to each team member.

"Wheels up, people." Walsh slammed a hand on the counter. "Let's go."

In a solemn but unwavering march, the team exited the house and loaded into three of the SUVs. Chance, Destiny and Bosco rode with Tiandra, Riker and Ammo in Walsh's SUV, and Graham and Skyler in her vehicle. They rumbled off the property in a single line and headed south, taking them into central Nebraska. Chance perched on the end of his seat, drumming his fingers on the dashboard.

He didn't stop until Tiandra put a hand on his bouncing leg. "You're killing me."

Chance glanced over at her, his hand paused in midair above the dashboard.

"If you don't stop that, I'm pulling this SUV over and tossing you into the dogs' kennel."

He winced. "Sorry, the drive is just taking forever."

"But we have a place to start. You're not in this fight alone. We all want to find Ayla."

"I know." But that wasn't enough. They had to rescue her before Sutler hurt her. And regardless, the twenty-four hours since her abduction meant time wasn't on their side or in their favor.

Common sense said they wouldn't find her at the cell's triangulated location, but he prayed it would produce a lead. "Can't we drive faster?"

Tiandra glanced over at him. "Not legally," she teased.

Chance tried to control his fidgeting in the seat, but by the time Graham announced, "We're almost there," over the team's dedicated police radio channel, he was crawling out of his skin with anxiety.

He visually scanned the area where the rolling hills had flattened to an endless landscape of cow pastures and cornfields. How had Ayla's phone pinged from here? And the thing no one else had mentioned was the intermittent cell phone reception they'd encountered. That meant Ayla's phone would've done the same and could've thrown off the location. No. He refused to think that way. Instead, Chance focused on the map, confirming they were in the right place.

Tiandra pulled onto a side lane, then turned onto a dirt road. She parked on the shoulder, the rest of the team following suit. Each hopped out, donning Kevlar vests, though the air was warm, and they likely wouldn't encounter the kidnapper. He was long gone. Chance shook off the thoughts. All they needed was a lead to help them find Ayla. He and Tiandra released the dogs, giving them time to shake off the drive before attaching their twenty-foot leashes and joining the rest of the team.

"The cell phone pinged around here, but that could mean a lot of things," Walsh said. "Let the K-9s handle the search. They're going to see things we can't." He addressed Chance. "Do you have Ayla's scent article?"

Chance held out Ayla's same nightshirt he had used before with Destiny. The soft material had absorbed her faint, floral aroma, taking him back to the last moments of holding her in his arms and the kiss that didn't happen. Scent was the closest link to memory, and it didn't fail to do its job. He sucked in a breath, determined to control his emotions. He knelt, allowing each dog to sniff the fabric. Destiny took the lead, but Ammo and Bosco were both cross-trained in locating lost or missing persons as well as criminal apprehension. With the trio, they had the best possible equipment needed to find Ayla.

Each handler spoke the same command: "Seek." The K-9s again sniffed the article, then turned and headed east.

The team stretched across the ground in a straight line and moved steadily in the grid search pattern.

"We have a triangulation of the area, not an absolute spot, so be watching for any clues," Skyler reminded the group.

Chance absorbed the mission. This was his element. Finding people, seeking fugitives. A flash of the first meeting with Ayla crossed his mind. *I'm not a fugitive. You are as far as I'm concerned.* He'd spoken callously to her, but truthfully, the response was the same. He sought the lost. Hadn't the Lord come to do the same? Chance had grown up in church, and he knew the stories and hymns, but those had been for Sunday morning. Yet he realized he longed for more than that. He needed God right now, in this place. As he gazed out into the vastness of the field, finding Ayla seemed impossible. *Lord, working past the impossible is Your specialty. Please do that now. Lead us to her.*

Destiny's pace increased, and Chance jogged to keep up. She paused. Then bolted forward again. In his peripheral vision he spotted Tiandra, Bosco, Riker and Ammo mimicking Destiny's actions.

They crossed the cornfield with the sun beating on them, the heat stifling except for the light breeze. The corn was high, ready for harvest, making it hard to see one another. He relied on the sounds of them tromping through the grounds, crunching stalks and earth, the panting of the dogs and swishing through the plants to indicate each person's location.

They exited the field, and the dogs paused, lifting their trained noses into the air. Then, in unison, the K-9s shifted slightly and hurried across the pasture toward a grove of old oak and cotton trees. Again, the team jogged to keep up with the intensity of the animals' pace. They entered the foliage, thick with overgrowth and brambles. A dove overhead cooed, annoyed by their disturbance, then flew off the branch where it had perched into the open field.

A knowing look passed between the team.

The dogs had found a scent.

"Destiny, seek," Chance commanded again. Tiandra and Riker ordered their dogs the same way.

Immediately she took off, her nose to the ground, Ammo and Bosco in line with her. They crossed the field to an adjacent dirt road, then continued into a pasture where golden prairie grass swayed with the breeze. The dogs moved through it, carving a path in the yellow sea, tails lifted high like beacons for their partners to follow.

Chance glanced over his shoulder. They'd walked a substantial distance. But Tiandra had said the location might exceed five miles in diameter.

At last, Destiny dropped to a sit and barked twice. Bosco and Ammo mimicked her move. The dogs' bodies were hidden by the swaying grass, leaving only their triangular ears peeking above. Chance bolted forward, outrunning Riker and Tiandra. He spotted the black cell phone, shattered, next to Destiny's right paw. The area showed signs of disturbance where the kidnapper probably drove.

"Don't touch it," Walsh hollered.

Chance stood still, battling the urge to reach down and grab the device.

Skyler hurried behind, already donning a latex glove from her cargo pants. She lifted the phone, collecting the pieces and placing them in a clear plastic bag, and passed it to Walsh.

Chance's stomach plummeted beneath his boots. He didn't need the confirmation. She'd been here.

"Is it hers?" Skyler asked.

Walsh nodded. "That's one of our phones."

Chance felt the weight of knowing Ayla had fought for her life here. She'd called his name and begged for help. Her cries had fallen to the ground, swept away without rescue. His chest constricted with a pain so intense it threatened to overwhelm him. In her bravery, she'd tried to fight back, and she'd given them a place to start looking for her. It wasn't enough, because as he turned, surveying the vast countryside, hopelessness consumed him. There wasn't a house or human in sight. They were miles from the road.

Now what?

A shrill whistle had them spinning around to see Tiandra waving them over. The team assembled around her.

"What's going on?" Chance asked.

"We have a new lead. State Patrol got a tip on a vehicle fire about two miles from here. The vehicle matches the description of the kidnapper's SUV," Walsh said.

"Shouldn't we keep searching here?" Chance asked.

"The dogs are locked. They haven't found a new scent," Riker argued.

"But they might."

"Negative. We need to follow up on the lead," Walsh ordered.

He was in no hurry to see a vehicle fire that left unpleasant images of burning evidence. If that was true, what would they find when they got there?

"Don't think about that," Riker said.

Chance jerked to look at him.

"It's written on your face," Riker explained. "We have a lead. Focus on that."

TEN

Groggy and disoriented, Ayla shivered against the cold cement penetrating through her thin shirt. She lay on her side and tried to sit up, then remembered her wrists were still bound. Her body ached from the fall into the root cellar, and she wondered if shock had overtaken her pain receptors. Maybe she had broken bones she'd not realized. At least her attacker hadn't taped her mouth again. She breathed in, and the air tasted heavy and earthy, a rotten mildew consuming her senses.

Engulfed in darkness, Ayla lifted her arms, unable to see them in front of her face. She scooted to a sitting position, and pain exploded in her leg, reminding her of the gunshot wound in her calf. Why hadn't she bled out? If only she could see the injury. She ran her fingers along the wet fabric. A through and through or had the bullet only grazed her skin? Touching the wound seemed to activate the nerve endings, causing her calf to throb with a fiery pain.

She leaned against the icy wall, acclimating herself to the area. A tickle against her neck caused her to react with an attempted and failed swipe. In the effort to battle whatever creature had crawled over her, she scraped her knuckles and wrenched her shoulder. Tears were close to the surface, but she refused to let them fall.

Water trickled from somewhere in the room, activating Ayla's thirst.

Bathed in darkness, she glanced up in search of any light source. She replayed the events from what she assumed occurred the night before.

The kidnapper's fury at her 9-1-1 call, and his comment about Sutler's harsh extraction methods lingered in her mind.

Rescue hadn't come. Her attempts had failed, leaving her survival a solo effort.

Optimism that she'd thrown off Sutler and bought herself time dwindled as she considered the hopelessness of her situation. "Please, Lord, send help." Her prayers hit the ceiling and dropped beside her. No one would come.

"Who's there?"

The familiar voice froze Ayla in place. Had she imagined the sound?

"Who's there?" the woman repeated.

"Octavia?" But how could it be? RJ's widow was supposed to be in South Carolina. How did she end up here?

"Ayla!"

She searched the darkness, unable to see the woman, but her voice was near.

"My ankles and wrists are bound. I can't move," Octavia said.

"He shot my leg, and my wrists are bound, too."

"Where are we?"

"A cellar in the middle of an abandoned farm."

Her jaw hurt from where the man had punched her, and one eye had swollen shut, restricting her vision. A cut on her lip and the taste of copper indicated he'd split the skin there.

"Your marshal was supposed to protect us from Sutler. I see he's done a great job of that."

Ayla recoiled, defensiveness rising. "You don't know what you're talking about."

"Don't I? Where are we? Certainly not somewhere safe."

"Keep your voice down," Ayla snapped.

"Why? Who's going to hear me? You oblivious girl! You're ignoring the truth because you're in love with that cop!"

Octavia's harshness wasn't new to Ayla, but she hadn't experienced her wrathful attitude in a long time. The return to her emotional past tightened her stomach with familiar responses from her childhood. In those days, Ayla's mother had intervened, absorbing the woman's venomous verbal attacks.

How had she forgotten that?

How long had she clouded over RJ and Octavia's behavior, sugarcoating the ugliness and viewing them through codependent, rose-colored glasses?

"Your visit to my house caused all of this," Octavia ranted. "All because you couldn't bear to be without your precious cellphone."

Immobilized by the verbal lashing, Ayla contemplated what to say. Was Octavia blaming her for RJ's murder? Of course she was. Ayla was the reason this nightmare had begun.

"How did you end up here?" Ayla asked.

"He kidnapped me and threatened to kill me if I don't produce that wretched list!"

"Myles Sutler," Ayla mumbled, looking up at where she assumed the cellar door was. She tried to stand, but her leg refused to bear the weight, and she dropped to the ground. "He brought you here?"

"Oh, yes, you know him well, right?"

Silence hung between them.

"I'm sorry, Ayla. I didn't mean to treat you that way.

I'm angry and frustrated, and I took it out on you. You've been through so much, and here I am flinging arrows."

Ayla lifted her chin. "It's okay. If I knew where that list was, I would have handed it over to him a long time ago."

"I feel the same way. How can I give him what he wants when I don't have a clue what or where it is? He talked to another man, and they agreed to do whatever it takes to get the information from us."

A shiver coursed through Ayla at the possibilities of what that meant.

"He said he'd start by making me watch you die. Ayla, he's going to kill us!"

"We must get out of here before Sutler returns. The fact we're both alive proves they believe we have the list. That's to our advantage," Ayla said.

"How so?"

"It'll buy us time. We need to convince them to get us out of here. Then we'll make a run for it." Ayla's mind raced, scouring her mental records for anything Ezra might've taught her that would help in this moment. And she came up empty. "We must escape. I need something to free my wrists first. Help me search."

"I can't even see you and you want me to find a weapon?" Octavia snapped. "And I can't move, remember?"

Ayla used the wall to push to a standing position, then hobbled forward. Her foot struck an object, and the sound of rattling glass caught her attention. A wooden shelving unit. She ambled along the front of it, her fingers searching for something that would pierce through tape.

A sharp nail head stuck out from the side of the shelf. Ayla stepped closer, positioning the nail between her wrists. She braced herself, putting her weight forward so as not to knock over the shelf. She pressed with all her might until the tape snapped, creating a small hole. Ayla repeated the process until the adhesive binding surrendered, and she separated her hands.

"I'm free."

"Then help me, too," Octavia demanded.

"Hold on," Ayla replied. Her hands roamed the shelf, grazing the sticky spiderwebs and layers of dust. Jars tinged as she shuffled the contents.

"What are you doing?" Octavia asked.

"Looking for a light source." Her fingers grazed a cylindrical object. She felt the small tip of a candle wick. "Yes!" She continued her touch search, locating a small box of matches. "Please work," she whispered as she struck one of the wooden matches against the flint. Four attempts and several sparks later, fire emerged.

"You did it!" Octavia praised.

Ayla lit the candle and, guarding the flame with her hand, turned slowly in search of Octavia.

She sat near the steps, hands bound behind her back and legs sprawled in front of her.

Though the cellar air was cool, sweat trickled down Ayla's forehead from the effort.

"Hurry!" Octavia ordered.

"Give me a second," Ayla snapped.

She gripped the post, waiting for the wave of pain in her leg to settle, then made her way across the confining space and knelt beside Octavia.

"I didn't believe him when he said you were down here." Streaks of black mascara streamed down Octavia's face. She had a busted lip and bruising over her cheeks and one eye.

Ayla remained silent, ripping the tape from Octavia's hands, then freeing her ankles. Then she turned her attention back to the shelves. Jars of what resembled tomatoes and pickles testified to someone's life here.

"What're you looking for?" Octavia asked, getting to her feet.

"We need a weapon. We'll attack Myles, then escape."

"Yes, that's good," Octavia nodded vehemently.

"Look for something we can use."

They scoured the cellar, looking for a weapon and an object large enough to ram the door. They found neither. Octavia attempted to push it open, but it didn't budge. From her bent position, she couldn't get the momentum needed, and Ayla's wounded leg prohibited her assistance. After what seemed like hours, they gave up.

They were stuck, and Sutler would kill them both. "We could hide and rush him," Ayla suggested.

Octavia looked up, tears streaking her face. "Do I look like a wrestler or a football player to you? I don't have that kind of strength." She smoothed her skirt, though her blouse remained ripped, and her hair swirled around her head in a disarray of curls. She'd broken off the heel of her pump, refusing to take off her shoes on the dirty floor.

"It's worth a try." Ayla crossed her arms over her chest. She lifted her eyes as though she could see through the door above.

"How? And then what? It'll get us killed," Octavia argued. "No way."

"You could distract him, and I'll attack," Ayla offered.

"If you fail and make them angry, it'll make things worse," Octavia argued. "Let's use our brains instead."

"I'm open to all your brilliant suggestions." Ayla's snarky reply, though out of character, seemed to surface a little too naturally. But Octavia refused to do anything more than complain. "Did you recognize the other man?"

"No, I asked his name, and that earned me this." Octavia pointed to her bruised lip. "I didn't press the issue."

"Ugh," Ayla groaned. "If only we had an advantage, like a normal door or window, to escape."

"I'm sure he'll let us walk right out." Octavia rolled her eyes.

"Okay let's work on a way to convince him we have to lead him to the list."

Octavia's expression cast doubt in Ayla's plan. Regardless, if Myles believed her, they had a chance. Stalling was their only hope of survival.

"I didn't believe RJ had the list, but I'm starting to wonder. He kept a lot of secrets. Although, if he'd hidden the list, you're the one he would've told."

Ayla blinked. "Why me?"

"Because he trusted you most." Octavia seemed to study her. "He did tell you, didn't he?" Her eyes widened. "I knew it! Although why you didn't just tell the authorities, I don't understand. But that is irrelevant now. You'll tell Myles, and he'll free us," Octavia rambled. "Although we could negotiate. He'd pay good money for that. Maybe we should bargain for something bigger."

Ayla gaped at her. Had the woman lost all sense of reality? "RJ did no such thing and hello! Once Myles has the list, he'll have no reason to keep us alive."

Octavia groaned. "Ezra brainwashed you."

At the words, Ayla's head snapped up. "Why do you say that? Did you know him?"

Octavia shrugged. "He tried to get me to talk to him or the authorities. He warned me Myles would come for me."

"So, what happened?"

"He urged me to go into witness protection, too." She waved her hand through the air dismissively. "I wasn't caving to his fear tactics. I told him everyone has a price and recommended he work that angle instead. Ezra's scruples cost him his life."

"Myles tried bribing Ezra, too?"

"Yes. If he'd taken the bribe, he'd be alive." Octavia shook her head. "Just like RJ. When does being honorable become being foolish? They're both dead, and for what?"

The last flickers of the candle went out, thrusting them back into the dark.

Ayla's instincts blared on high alert, and for the first time, she saw Octavia in a different light and knew she was on her own.

"We will find her. Have faith," Riker said, approaching Chance once they exited the vehicles. They stood some distance from the fire site at the end of an open field near the barn where authorities had found the burned vehicle.

"What's that mean?" Chance hated voicing his vulnerability, but discouragement had taken over the facade he'd worn to look good in front of his team. "Nothing I've done has worked."

"Faith means trusting God alone, not our own abilities."

"What if He fails?" The words escaped before Chance could stop them, but the question was one of the truest fears of his heart. After all, God had failed Chance and Shelton the day the gang members had attacked them. He'd failed to protect Marissa and Ayla. "No offense, but God doesn't have a stellar track record with me. How can I trust God when He keeps letting me down?"

"Look, man, I get what you're saying, and I've been there, feeling like God has turned His back on you when things look hopeless," Riker said, leading the way down the path. "He's always working, and even when we don't understand, God is putting everything together for a better plan."

"That's just something we say to make ourselves feel better." Chance snorted.

"Maybe." Riker shrugged. "I just know that if we could figure everything out, we wouldn't need God. The midnight hour is when He does His greatest work and reminds us He's the one in control."

"So why does He let bad things happen?"

"Dude, that's a question so far above my pay grade that I can't fathom the answer. And really, I'm not sure it would make you feel better anyway." Riker ran a hand through his hair as he seemed to struggle with an explanation. "Humans have the right to free will, and centuries of wars, murder and other heinous acts have proven we take that free will to the extreme. Then we blame God when things go wrong. We also try to take credit for all the good things, as though God had nothing to do with those. But you don't see folks shaking their fists at Him when things go well."

Chance considered the argument, though he didn't comment.

"But what I can say for certain is that I've watched God move in ways I never expected, even when it's taken me down hard paths, testing my resolve to the core. And in the end, God showed me things about myself and took me to the point where I thought it was hopeless, only to demonstrate His sovereignty in the situation. Without God's hand in my life, I'd never have met Eliana, and we wouldn't have her DNA-phenotyping system to help with our cases. I'd never have known the truth about my birth mom and twin."

The story of Riker finding his twin was like a movie of the week, and the team spoke of it often. "The same brother who tried to kill you?" Chance was being a jerk, but he couldn't help it. Frustration boiled over within him and he was tired of placating conversations about a God who didn't seem to care about what was happening to Ayla.

"One and the same. All that changed my life, and the truth is, I'd do it again just to meet and marry Eliana. Loving her is worth every rotten thing it took to get to her."

"I love her," Chance blurted. But would he ever get to tell Ayla?

"I'm assuming you mean Ayla, not Eliana?" Riker teased.

The comment lightened the moment slightly. "Yeah. I can't believe I just admitted that to you."

"What? You think the team hasn't already figured it out?"

Warmth radiated up Chance's neck. "You did?"

"Dude, we're trained observers. Plus, you have the most telltale face I've ever seen."

Chance winced. "Ayla says my expressions are too evident." His throat tightened at the reminder of her words.

"We need to fix that. You'll stink at undercover work if you can't control your face."

Chance kicked at a rock. "Yeah, maybe in my next job I'll have that opportunity."

Riker gripped his arm. "Whoa. You're thinking of leaving HFTF?"

"Not voluntarily. Ever since I heard about you all, I've wanted to be a part of this team. But after all the ways I've messed up and showed my incompetency, Walsh is going to fire me for sure."

"Dude, are you really thinking Walsh will boot you off the team?"

"Why shouldn't he? I've blown it at every turn. I let Ayla down." And then it hit Chance. He'd blamed God for the events when in reality, he'd botched the assignment.

"Have you given this battle over to God?" Riker asked.

"What?"

"You're clenching it too tightly. Like handing God a toy

and asking Him to fix it, then yanking it away again and saying, 'I'll do it myself.'"

"I haven't had time to think about all that." But he had. And Riker was right. He'd blamed God for not taking care of anything, but he never really trusted Him to handle it, either. He stopped, leaning against a split rail fence, and bowed his head. *Lord, I'm sorry. I know this isn't on You. But I need You to rescue her, even if I can't be a part of it.* The prayer was heartfelt and more honest than Chance had ever been in his life.

"He knows your heart."

"Riker, I'd do anything to bring Ayla home safely. I'd exchange my life for hers."

"Let's hope it doesn't come to that."

Walsh's voice roared over their headsets, interrupting their conversation. "Fire is out. We can approach," Walsh announced. "Firefighters have cleared the premises for us to work."

The handlers released their K-9s, leashing them and preparing for a search with the scent article. Firefighters loaded their hoses and equipment.

Again, working in a grid pattern, the team spread out, flashlights in hand and dogs taking the lead.

Through the overgrown fields, the dilapidated barn came into view. The building appeared to be on its last legs, leaning precariously to the side, though whether it had looked that way prior to the fire, Chance wasn't sure. Destiny jerked the leash, nearly ripping it from his hand. If she moved with that kind of speed, she'd found something.

Destiny tried to move into the barn that smelled of smoke, rotting grain and other things he'd rather not think about.

They approached with caution. The vehicle sat, blackened by the fire, and dripping from the fire hoses.

Chance swallowed hard. *Please don't let Ayla be here.*

They surrounded the SUV, glancing warily at the structure overhead.

"The kidnapper must've realized we could trace the call," Tiandra said, sweeping her beam over the burned car.

"Yeah, but why ditch the vehicle?" Skyler asked.

Walsh moved around the SUV. "Plates are gone." He reached for the door handle. "It's locked."

They had probable cause since the SUV matched the description of the kidnapper's vehicle. Walsh lifted his flashlight and shattered the passenger window, then unlocked the door. He tugged it wide and reached into the glove box. No documents of ownership. They scoured the vehicle for the engraved vehicle identification numbers, only to find them scratched out.

The kidnapper had ensured they wouldn't be able to trace the vehicle easily. Chance moved to the rear door and tugged it open, holding his breath.

He exhaled at the empty interior. Destiny moved beside him, again sitting and barking twice to indicate she'd tracked Ayla's scent.

Skyler's phone rang, and she quickly answered, holding up a finger to the group to let them know she'd need a minute.

They continued surveying the vehicle for any clues while Skyler exited the barn, speaking in a low tone.

"Nada." Riker walked to Chance.

"Same here. Between the fire damage and the effort in concealing the owner, I've got nothing."

The team stepped outside. Chance surveyed the barn in the center of an abandoned pasture. The kidnapper had chosen this place intending to desert the vehicle. He'd deviated from his original plan, which meant Ayla had thrown him off his game. And he'd burned it hoping to hide evidence, maybe only the scent of Ayla, but he'd feared they'd trace the car. That meant something. And the divergence from this plan had bought the team time to find her.

"Let's head back and regroup," Walsh said.

"Skyler and I will work on finding the owner of the SUV," Riker said, tossing Chance his keys. "We'll meet you guys at the Rock."

The group dispersed, and Chance loaded Destiny into the truck.

Chance's radio came to life.

"My friend at the FBI cleaned up the footage from your ranch, Commander," Skyler announced. "He got an ID on the kidnapper's vehicle. Octavia Warden is the registered owner."

Chance processed the information. He joined the conversation. "But the kidnapper was male."

"Is she the victim or working with Sutler?" Walsh asked.

"Or she's the CI who worked with Ezra," Riker inserted.

"What advantage would Octavia have not to go into WitSec if she wanted to be a CI?" Tiandra asked.

"Tiandra's right," Chance said. "The little interaction I had with Octavia didn't leave me with the impression of a bold, fierce spy and confidential informant. Besides, she was going to stay with her family on the East Coast." Why was he arguing the point?

"And we escorted her to the airport," Riker said.

"I'll make some calls to verify she made the flight," Tiandra replied.

Chance tapped the steering wheel. "I think we should return to where Destiny found the phone."

"Negative," Walsh replied.

"There's a flight from Des Moines to South Carolina with Octavia's name," Tiandra inserted. "But she's not listed on the manifest."

"She never made the flight," Skyler said.

"Octavia is in danger!" Chance replied. "Ayla worried that would happen."

"Sutler could've abducted Octavia. He'd pit them against each other," Riker said.

"We'll keep the discussion going at the Rock," Walsh replied.

"I'm on my way, but I need a few to regroup," Chance said.

"Don't take too long," Walsh replied.

Chance held back, allowing the team to proceed ahead of him, ensuring they wouldn't see him returning to the phone's pinged location. His mind raced, and before he realized it, he shifted into Park beneath a canopy of tree cover. Again, he debated notifying the team. No. Walsh would order him to stand down if Chance confessed his plans. Most likely they'd fire him once the case was over anyway.

Chance knew how to track fugitives, and his instincts said to dig deeper here.

He couldn't take his phone. They'd trace his location. He turned it off, then placed it in the console.

He parked and released Destiny. "All right, let's try this again."

Chance and Destiny continued working the area. The dog sniffed the air, then shifted, increasing her pace. Chance jogged to keep up with her.

They descended into a valley and creek separated by a thick tree line. He stumbled into the tepid water and lost his balance, catching himself on a log. In the dark, he struggled to see the ground, but he didn't want to hinder Destiny's search.

Chance's flashlight swept across the ground, unable to keep up with the dog's fierce trailing.

They crested the hill into a pasture, and headlights beamed on the road ahead. The vehicle faded from sight.

Destiny lunged forward, determined in her search. He should call for backup, but the shepherd strained at the end of her leash. They jogged through the pasture, and Chance spotted the structure ahead. An old farmhouse.

He reached for his cell phone, remembering he'd left it behind and instantly regretting the decision. At least he still had his Glock.

They approached the house, reaching a wire mesh fence where Destiny paused, sniffing furiously before launching over it. Chance's climb wasn't as graceful, but they continued moving. He withdrew his Glock. A soft glow illuminated from behind the window. If the vehicle he'd seen had been here, was anyone still inside?

Chance drew Destiny close and gave her the hand gestures for a silent approach.

Destiny licked his hand, then took off, rounding the house.

Where was she going?

The shepherd aimed for the back side of the house and moved to the hatch doors of a cellar. Chance knelt in front of the door, inspecting the padlock that secured the latch. He needed something to break it off.

Chance flicked a glance at the house, contemplating where to look first. If someone was inside, he'd be an open target in the cellar. He had to check for the assailant first. He tugged Destiny back, and they approached the door.

Chance and Destiny climbed the steps to the rotting porch, leaning unsteadily. Chance reached for the doorknob, surprised it was unlocked. He gave it a cautious push, and the door swung open, releasing a musty aroma that mingled with damp carpet and mildew.

They stepped inside, Chance's boots crunching on the

floor. An old, yellowed couch sat beneath the window covered in foil and draped by floral curtains that hung askew. Pizza boxes and fast-food wrappers cluttered the space, and the steel coffee table held cardboard cups and ashtrays filled to overflowing.

They entered the kitchen. The single counter held stacks of dishes caked in rotten food. To his right, a bathroom emitted the scent of urine. Based on the toilet lying on its side, the facilities weren't functional. He searched for a phone line but found none. Not surprising, since the house didn't appear to be inhabitable. More like a place for squatters.

He found nothing but a similar mess in the other rooms. They exited, and Destiny again dragged him to the cellar. Chance turned, spotting the small gardening shed, and rushed to it, locating an old iron shovel. He positioned the tool and tugged, breaking the lock free.

ELEVEN

Rapid scratching caught Ayla's attention. "Shh!"

Octavia's eyes widened at the rebuke, but to her credit, she quieted.

"Listen."

Again, she heard movement from above, and a sliver of light appeared from between the door boards.

No voices. The darkness perpetuated Ayla's fear and confusion.

Then a slam.

Octavia gasped a little too loudly, and Ayla glared at her. Though what difference would it make now? If Myles stood outside those doors, they were already dead.

The delay left her heart pounding through her throat.

Who was there?

Ayla prayed it was rescue coming, but the possibility that Myles Sutler or the kidnapper had returned sent a shiver up her spine.

"He's coming back!" Octavia hissed.

Ayla moved in the direction of the shelf, steadying herself and grabbing jars of canned vegetables in each hand. She adjusted her pose, ready to pitch them at the intruder. Her grip tightened, and she flicked a glance at the ceiling. Running up the stairs with her injured leg wasn't an option. She looked down at her food weapons.

What was she doing?

Buying time. Any distraction helped.

Resolved to fight her way out of the cellar, she watched the door for movement.

Several seconds passed without another sound.

The doors swung open, and a bright beam swept over the stairs. A flashlight.

Had help arrived?

Caught between crying out and remaining quiet, Ayla contemplated what to do. She gripped the jars tighter, struggling to keep her stance with her injured leg.

"Help!" Octavia screamed.

Ayla whipped her neck toward the woman. She flicked another glance at the steps. No response.

"Help us!" Octavia cried.

No turning back now. Ayla joined in the pleas. "Help! Down here!"

The scratching returned, then a familiar canine whimper.

"Destiny?" Ayla cried.

"Ayla?" Chance's voice reached her like a lifeline.

The shepherd bounded down the stairs, greeting Ayla with wet kisses. She dropped the jars, and they landed with a *thunk* on the dirt floor.

Chance tromped down the steps and consumed the confining space with his muscular frame. He paused at the base where Octavia sat, then swung his flashlight to the corner where Ayla bent over, one hand clinging to the shelf, the other wrapped in Destiny's furry coat.

"Hungry?" he teased, gesturing toward the jars.

Ayla glanced down and laughed. She rose and reached for him, wobbling a little. "Chance!"

He crossed the space in one stride, pulling her close. Ayla inhaled his comforting, musky scent.

"Shh. I don't know when he'll return. Keep your voices low," Chance advised. "Let's get out of here."

Ayla leaned back. "I can't walk that far. He shot my leg."

Chance surveyed the injury with the flashlight. "There's entrance and exit wounds, so I'm guessing it's a through and through, but you're bleeding pretty good. I'm surprised you didn't pass out."

"I did. Several times."

"I have nothing to bandage you with here. I'll carry you up and we'll deal with it once we're away from this place."

"No arguments here."

"Okay." He cradled Ayla, allowing her to wrap her arms around his neck.

"You came for me," she whispered, melting against his chest, enveloped in his embrace.

"Of course I did. You're my fugitive." His breath was soft against her ear like a warm summer breeze.

"Hello? What about me?" Octavia whined, jerking them to the present.

Ayla tried not to roll her eyes.

"Do you have any injuries?" Chance asked.

"Well, he beat me up." The woman's voice was thick with neediness.

"Can you walk on your own?"

"Yes, I suppose," she huffed.

"Great. Okay, stay close and follow me." Chance turned. "Destiny, heel." The dog immediately moved to his side.

They climbed from the cellar, and Ayla caught Octavia's less than impressed glower as she trailed behind. Once they were aboveground, they crept to the shadows beside an old gardening shed. Chance gently set Ayla down. "There's no one here, but I saw headlights driving away earlier."

"Was it Myles and the guy who kidnapped me?" Ayla asked.

"Possibly." Chance peered toward the road. "I didn't get a good look from where I was."

"Where are the police?" Octavia looked around, hands on her hips. "Where's your vehicle?"

A frown crossed Chance's face. "We'll have to walk back to my truck."

"Don't you have a cell phone?" Octavia snapped.

"No. Long story."

"How far away are you parked?" Ayla asked.

He winced. "Too far." Chance helped Ayla to her feet, and she gripped his arm, teetering unsteadily. "I'll slow you down. Go for help, or your truck, and come back for me."

"Yes, let's do that," Octavia replied.

Chance shook his head. "No way. I'm not leaving you."

"But I can't walk through the fields like this."

Something she couldn't quite describe passed over Chance's handsome face. He glanced at the house. "We can't stick around here. I'll just carry you."

Headlights beamed from the road.

"They're coming back!" Octavia cried. The woman had an indisputable way of stating the obvious, as though it helped the situation.

Destiny growled, standing guard in front of them. Chance snapped on her leash and silenced her with a whispered, "Shh." Then he attached the leash to a D-ring on his belt and addressed Octavia. "We don't have the luxury of light, so be careful where you step."

She *harrumphed*, but to Chance's credit, he didn't acknowledge the attitude. "Let's go!" He hefted Ayla into his arms, and they moved through the yard, keeping to the shadows. When they reached the wire mesh fence, Destiny leaped over, easily clearing the top. Chance set Ayla down on the other side before helping Octavia over. He crossed it in one swift move, but the process took too long for Ayla's comfort.

The vehicle pulled up to the house and parked, nearly illuminating their location with the headlights.

Urgency sent Ayla's pulse rushing through her veins.

Chance whipped her into his arms and bolted, Destiny and Octavia keeping in stride. Each jostling of her leg blasted pain through Ayla. She clenched her teeth to keep from crying out.

Chance carried her with ease, though Ayla knew her added weight hindered their pace. Octavia moved quickly, and Destiny led the way.

They paused in the pasture behind the enormous cylindrical bales. Octavia pressed a hand to her chest, heaving with exertion. "You're lucky he's carrying you."

As if Ayla had chosen to be shot. She shook her head, unwilling to engage in the meaningless conversation.

Chance peered around the bale, then turned to face them. "They're sweeping the house, so they've discovered you've escaped. We must keep moving."

Again, the group barreled into the night, running as fast as the uneven ground and darkness allowed. Raised voices reached them, but the distance prevented Ayla from hearing the exact words spoken. Regardless, it was clear Myles and the kidnapper had returned to an unexpected situation, and they weren't pleased.

Ayla refused to look back, pressed against Chance's chest, his heavy breaths and heartbeat adding to her angst.

A gunshot exploded in the night, echoing on the wind.

Octavia screamed.

"There!" a male voice exclaimed in the distance.

No. No. This wasn't happening. They were so close to freedom. *God, help us!*

Rustling behind them indicated the men were following.

"Destiny, heel," Chance ordered, tugging her backward.

Ayla prayed the dog stayed beside them. The men wouldn't hesitate to shoot her.

Gunshots pierced the air, and she ducked closer into Chance's chest.

"They're right behind us!" Octavia cried.

"Get to the next bale," Chance ordered.

The rapid gunfire compounded the already extensive distance. At last, they rounded the large bale and ducked behind it for shelter. Chance set Ayla down on her feet, and she braced herself against the stiff hay.

Octavia whimpered, peering around the other side. "They're coming."

Ayla inched closer to look over the woman's shoulder. Lights bounced in the distance, moving toward them. She faced Chance. "We can't outrun them." He withdrew his gun, checking the magazine, and returned fire.

Bullets hit the bale, and Ayla ducked, covering her head. Octavia dropped beside her, mimicking her pose.

After several minutes, the shots ceased.

Ayla looked up. Chance still peered around the hay bale, but he remained still.

"Are they gone?" she asked him.

"Not sure," he whispered.

Ayla rose, gripping the straw for stability. She peered around the bale, spotting light bouncing in the distance, away from the house. "They're leaving?"

"Yeah. I don't like it," Chance said, holstering his gun.

"Then shouldn't we go to the house and call for help?" Octavia asked.

"There isn't a phone there," Chance told her. "Or I would have called long ago."

Octavia huffed and crossed her arms. "Well, we can't stay out here."

"No. I'm parked in the clearing. We need to get to the SUV."

"But they'll find us on the road," Octavia argued.

"No. It's near a minimum maintenance road. We're close."

"Fine," Octavia grumbled.

Ayla bit back the smart retort lingering on her lips. Chance hefted her into his arms again, and a spark of what Ayla could only describe as jealousy passed over Octavia's face, fading as quickly as it appeared.

They continued the trek through the tall grass into the valley, where the creek and trees offered a reprieve.

"We're almost there. You're doing great," Chance encouraged Octavia.

She nodded, still panting from the effort. Sympathy for the woman overwhelmed Ayla, and she chastised herself for the harsh way she'd viewed Octavia. *Help me grant her the mercy and kindness she needs, Lord.* Ayla reached for her hand, giving it a squeeze and earning a grateful quiver of a smile.

Soon they crested the hill. Ayla nearly cried out at the sight of the familiar task force SUV parked beside the tree line.

"We're almost there," Chance assured.

They were a few feet away when a car skidded between them and the SUV, enveloping them in a dust cloud. Destiny barked, lunging for the vehicle, but Chance gripped her leash, restricting her. The dog reluctantly but quickly obeyed, moving to his side.

Chance set Ayla down and shifted protectively in front of her and Octavia. "Stay behind me."

The darkened window lowered, and Myles Sutler leaned out, wielding a huge gun. "I thought you'd never get here."

Ayla gasped at the fully automatic weapon.

Destiny resumed barking and snapping. Rapid gunfire and the flashes of light from the rounds sent Ayla diving for the ground. Dirt exploded around her in small bursts, showing where the bullets hit the ground.

She glanced up to see Chance shielding her and Destiny. Octavia crouched behind Ayla.

"You move fast." Myles laughed, getting out of the car. His headlights illuminated the area.

As though her mind needed confirmation Myles Sutler stood before her, Ayla's gaze traveled to the ugly tattoo on the criminal's neck. Yes. Definitely Myles.

"Next time, I'll aim for all of you."

Ayla got to her feet with Octavia's help. "What do you want?" She pushed ahead of Chance.

"I want what you're hiding from me," Myles replied.

"Okay, let's talk this out." Chance placed a hand on her shoulder, again shifting protectively in front of her.

"Save your negotiator talk. Get into the car, Ayla," Myles ordered.

"No." Octavia gripped her arm.

"She's not going anywhere," Chance said.

He only wanted her, so he'd spare Chance and Octavia if she cooperated. Ayla fixed her gaze on the sedan's dark-tinted windows, restricting her view of the passenger side and back seat. Was there anyone else in the car? The idea settled, giving her courage.

Destiny continued snapping and barking, stretching to the full extent of the leash Chance allowed her.

Myles raised the gun. "Shut that dog up before I silence it permanently."

Ayla shifted closer to Myles, putting herself between the man and dog. "Chance, put the dog in the kennel," she said loudly, withholding the shepherd's name purposely.

"No. I'll just eliminate the mutt," Myles replied. "Get out of the way, Ayla."

Myles fired a shot, pinging the dirt next to Octavia and eliciting her scream.

"Stop!" Ayla balanced on her good leg, searching her mind for anything she could do to stop the situation. Myles believed she had the list. Now his insistence and delusional thinking were her only weapon. In that moment, she realized nothing else mattered except Chance, Octavia and Destiny's survival. "I'm not telling you anything until you let all of them go. Unharmed."

"Ayla, no!" Chance blurted. What was she doing?

"Put the dog in the kennel," Sutler demanded. "Drop your gun and kick it to me."

Chance withdrew his weapon, contemplating the options. He'd get a shot in, but if Myles shifted, Chance risked hitting Ayla. He dropped the gun and kicked it to the man then reached for Destiny's leash. They moved toward the SUV, and he opened the back door to the kennel, ordering the dog inside. He closed the door, praying it wasn't the last time he saw his partner alive. The steel hindered Destiny's desperate whimpers and scratches.

"Come here." Sutler gestured to Octavia, whimpering like a child. "You're going to tie up the nice marshal," he said, passing her a set of zip ties.

"No, Sutler, you do it," Chance taunted. All he needed was Sutler to let go of Ayla and give him a chance to tackle the criminal.

"Give me some credit. She's going to do it for me while I stand here with your girlfriend." Sutler snaked an arm around Ayla's neck, tugging her backward. She stumbled, her neck catching on his forearm, and righted herself. He pressed the tip of the gun against her skull.

Chance lunged, and Sutler fired, hitting the driver's door. "Stay where you are."

The blast halted Chance. Blood boiling in anger, he withheld his fury, absorbing every ounce of his restraint. "Let her go!"

Octavia turned, blinking.

Sutler hollered, "Move!" The order sent the woman scurrying to Chance.

He placed his hands in front, and Myles roared with laughter. "You can't be serious. Behind your back!"

Chance glowered, doing as Sutler ordered. Octavia inched around him as though he'd spontaneously burst into flames. With his hands out of Sutler's view, Chance intertwined his fingers, leaving as much room as possible between his wrists without making it obvious. Octavia secured the zip ties, then scurried away when she'd finished the task.

"Now check his pockets, remove his cell phone and make sure he doesn't have any other weapons," Sutler ordered.

A knowing look passed between Ayla and Chance. Octavia would discover the extra knives he carried. Would she conceal them?

"And if you miss any, I'll make sure you pay for your incompetence," Sutler added.

Octavia nodded, moving faster this time, and did as he instructed. "There's no phone," she declared.

"Where is it?" Sutler demanded. Ayla winced in his constricting hold.

"In the console," Chance confessed.

Octavia retrieved the device and tossed it, then removed his pocketknife hidden in the large cargo pant pocket, finishing with the Leatherman tucked in his tactical duty belt. *Please don't let her check my boot.*

"That's all," she announced, passing them to Sutler. He tossed them into the tree line.

Chance forced himself to keep a nonchalant expression.

"Where is your friend? The impostor firefighter kidnapper?" Ayla asked, no doubt stalling.

Destiny continued barking, her yelps like threatening pleas.

"He failed by letting you escape. So, I rid myself of the mess," Sutler said, as leisurely as reporting the weather. "Next, I'll eliminate you, good marshal, and your mutt. You should've stayed with your team. There's strength in numbers and all that. Don't they teach you those important factors?" He guffawed.

"I'll talk. But not until you let them go."

"Hmm." Sutler tapped the gun against her head in a light, mocking gesture. "If only I believed you. If they're here, I have assurance you'll do what you say."

"Then we're at an impasse, because I'm not talking until you do what I've asked."

Chance shifted his feet. Would the team arrive if they stalled long enough?

"Talk or they die!" Sutler demanded.

"No! Ayla, just tell him," Octavia pleaded.

"I'm not saying a word until you promise me I get something out of this." A knowing look passed between Ayla and Chance.

"She has a point there, Sutler," Chance said. "Better give her something to bargain with."

"Hmm, all right. You give me the list and I'll have what I need to disappear until this all blows over."

"Blows over? Are you kidding?" This time, Chance guffawed. "You're a fugitive. The marshals won't stop hunting you."

"Oh, but they will. See, that's the great thing about the list. Having it buys me the connections I need for my freedom. Outs the people I want and makes them do my bidding."

Ayla hung her head as though processing the words.

Sutler's proclamation was accurate, as much as Chance hated to admit it. The Heartland Fugitive Task Force would never give up on hunting him, but they were subject to bosses, too. If they called off the search, what choice would the team have? Once Sutler secured the list, ensuring it didn't fall into the wrong hands, he had power.

"Whoever is on that list will kill you if you don't find it," Chance replied. "You've put them into danger, and they won't have that."

A strange expression crossed Sutler's face. He leaned over Ayla's shoulder. "You can see why I can't stop until I get what I want."

"You're a victim, too," Ayla replied.

Chance recognized her ploy—using compassion to keep Sutler off guard.

"We're all servants to a master," Sutler replied.

"Yes, we are. And we choose whom we'll serve," Ayla replied.

Chance started to speak, but the peace that settled on her face kept him silent. She was working a plan. He just wasn't sure what.

Sutler snorted. "Or it's chosen for us."

"Not if our faith rests in God," Ayla said. "He's the only one deserving of our loyalty."

A shadow passed over Sutler's face. "If you really believe that, you're stupider than I thought."

"Maybe." She shrugged. "Or I'm right. Either way, there's no reason for you to hold Chance here."

"What about me?" Octavia gasped.

"Where would we run?" Ayla asked. "Going to the police is useless, since we don't know who is working for you. And even in witness protection, we're unsafe."

The comment stung Chance with the pain of a thousand

wasps. Defeat threatened to take him to his knees. He had to do something, and fast.

Ayla offered him an almost imperceptible shake of her head.

"You're absolutely right." A smug smile passed over Sutler's face. "There's no place to hide from me."

"Tell him what he wants, so he'll let us go!" Octavia bellowed.

"She's right." Sutler's words dripped with deception.

"Okay. Let her go." Ayla gestured at Octavia. "If she knew anything, she'd have said so by now."

"Exactly!" Octavia nodded vehemently.

Chance frowned. The woman clearly only cared about herself.

Sutler seemed to consider the offer. "She'd be in the same predicament, so to speak. If she steps out of line, I'll hunt her down and eliminate her."

Octavia's swallow was audible from where Chance stood, and she returned to whimpering.

"Right. I'll do what you want," Ayla injected. "But no harm can come to Chance, his dog or Octavia."

"I suppose that works." Sutler focused his cold-blooded stare at Chance.

He'd never allow Chance to live. "He's a liar, Ayla!"

"I said I would." Sutler reached over Ayla's shoulder, sweeping his gun past Chance to Destiny's kennel in the SUV. "It'd be a shame to kill such a beautiful animal. Worse if you had to watch, right, Marshal?"

"No!" Ayla gasped. "Myles, I believe you. Let them go."

"Let's compromise. Marshal, get into the kennel with your dog."

"What?" Chance blinked. "No way."

Sutler fired, striking the bottom of the rear driver's side door. "The next one won't miss."

Chance scowled.

"Hop in there." Sutler grinned. "Octavia, open the door for the nice man."

Octavia hurried to do what Sutler ordered, then paused. "What if the dog comes out?"

"Then I'll be forced to kill it." He shrugged. "Understand?"

"Please, Chance, just do what he says," Ayla pleaded, offering a wink.

Confusion cluttered Chance's mind. What was she doing? "I'll make sure she stays." He moved closer. "Heel!"

The shepherd's barking and scratching ceased. Chance nodded, and Octavia opened the door, allowing him to slide inside. She slammed it shut behind him.

Destiny whimpered, licking his face.

"I know, girl, get ready. We'll take care of that jerk," Chance assured.

Time to even the score.

Muffled voices, a strange sound at the back of the SUV, then the car engine started. They were leaving!

Chance shifted to sit on his knees and worked to get the knife from his boot. The engine revved and faded. Frantically, he retrieved the knife, pressing the button to open the blade. Then he positioned the blade and sawed through the zip ties.

"Come on!"

One zip tie broke.

Destiny whimpered, facing the rear of the kennel.

She barked twice and sat. Indicating. Chance surveyed the kennel, still sawing at the remaining zip tie. What was she focused on?

At last, the plastic snapped free.

Chance paused.

Two muffled beeps sounded from the back of the SUV. A bomb!

TWELVE

Ayla felt the explosion before she heard the boom. "No! You promised you'd let Chance go!" Tears stung her eyes, and her wrists were bound behind her back. She wriggled in the seat, desperate to free herself.

"Thanks for setting up your marshal for me." Sutler's sardonic laughter filled the car. "Once he was in the kennel, he never saw the bomb coming."

No. It couldn't be true. She'd surrendered with the intention of saving Chance and Destiny. Ayla remembered he wore the kennel remote door control on his belt, which provided a means of escape. The small box was nearly imperceptible to anyone unfamiliar with it. Assured he'd come for her, she prayed he'd understand. She hadn't counted on Sutler's forward thinking. Once more, he'd won the battle.

"Just in case you're thinking of clamming up, remember I still have your friend Octavia hostage, too."

As if emphasizing the dark image, Octavia whimpered.

Scenarios raced in Ayla's mind caught somewhere between helpless sorrow at Chance and Destiny's demise and rage against Myles. The pain overwhelmed her heart and Ayla forced it back. She was no stranger to loss, and she welcomed the familiar numbness that allowed her to breathe. She would not let Myles win. Now she'd fight back. For Chance.

Battle options countered the images of Chance that fought for her focus.

She could throw her legs over the seat and strangle Myles as he drove. Except her wounded leg throbbed, and without freeing her hands, they might die in the car accident surely to follow. If she ran with her injured leg, how far would she get? She groaned, aware she couldn't leave Octavia.

Chance and Destiny were dead.

Because of her.

Again, thoughts of them tore at her heart. What had she done? She'd hoped to give them the opportunity to escape. Instead, she'd led them to their deaths. Her chest tightened, threatening to cut off her air supply.

The car slowed and stopped. "Okay. Now you're going to tell me where the list is."

"Just kill me and get it over with," Ayla replied.

Octavia sniveled, protesting beneath the tape covering her mouth.

"I don't think your friend agrees," Myles said.

Ayla sighed, allowing her head to droop forward. Myles would kill them both. She'd known that from the start but sacrificing herself for Chance had made her brave. Even if she told Myles where the list was—not that she knew— he'd kill Octavia, too. What difference did it make?

"You will tell me." The door opened, then another door. Octavia cried out, and the weight on the seat shifted.

"Don't hurt her!" *Lord, give me wisdom. What do I do?* She needed to get to a phone or computer. She'd find the list and ensure it got into the hands of HFTF. Ayla would vindicate Chance. The idea percolated, and she blurted, "I don't know exactly where it is. I need Octavia's help!" Ayla emphasized the word *exactly*.

A shuffling. Octavia cried out, then the weight of her

return to the seat, and the door slammed. She shot Ayla a tearful glance. Myles had removed the tape from her mouth.

"Good." A few seconds later, the driver's door shut, and the car shifted into motion again.

"What do you mean?" Octavia sniffled. "I don't know where it is."

"RJ would've most likely hidden the list at your house, right?" Ayla directed her question at Octavia.

"But they've already gone through my house and haven't found anything."

"Maybe they didn't know where to look," Ayla contended.

"That's where he kept all his valuables," Octavia said, as though processing the information.

"You confronted RJ and killed him at his house," Ayla addressed Myles. "You believe it's there, too. But you didn't know him like we do." She lifted her chin defiantly. "I'll find it for you."

"Where?" Suspicion hung in Myles's tone.

"I'll have to go there myself." Ayla's boldness grew. "Make your choice. You won't find it without me, and I can't tell you where to look. RJ always enjoyed setting up treasure hunts for my brother and me. I have a feeling he used that same idea for the list."

"Yes!" Octavia bounced on the seat in excitement. "RJ loved those."

"You didn't have to kill him," Ayla said softly, glancing out the window.

"Yeah, I did," Myles said with a snort.

Ayla shifted in the seat, catching sight of Octavia from the corner of her eye. The woman's arms were still bound behind her back, but her expression softened to one of understanding. "I'm so sorry, honey."

Ayla averted her eyes, filling with tears.

Could she trust Octavia? Surely if she was working with Myles, they'd discontinue this charade. Yet the woman sat beside her, facing the same fate. As if hearing her internal debate, Octavia began to cry. Wails so heart wrenching they tore at Ayla's heart. No, Octavia was a victim, too.

The force of the explosion had thrust the back end of the SUV into the air, and it dropped to the ground with the intensity of a meteor hitting the earth. Chance and Destiny had escaped just in time and sat watching from a distance as the flames consumed the vehicle. He'd searched for his cell phone and found it shattered on the rocks. So much for calling in reinforcements. Once the fire settled down, they ran to the smoldering vehicle.

Chance peered through the broken driver's window. A hole where the radio had been indicated that wasn't an option, either.

"Lord, please help Ayla," he prayed aloud. Destiny whined, pacing with him.

The SUV continued to smoke, and they walked away.

A second explosion rocked the earth. Chance glanced over his shoulder. Had he and Destiny looked for the radio even a few moments later, they'd be dead for sure. They made their way toward the road and spotted headlights rounding the corner.

Was Sutler coming back to finish them?

Chance tugged Destiny's leash, and they ran into the tree line, seeking shelter. Behind the cover of the thick evergreen, he exhaled relief at the familiar sight of the HFTF vehicles. "Help has arrived," he informed the shepherd.

They hurried to meet his team as the SUVs skidded to a stop.

Riker exited first, glancing at the demolished SUV. "I can see what happened. Where's Ayla?"

Chance gave a concise explanation as the other members joined them. "I don't know where he took them. How'd you find me?"

"When you didn't show up at the Rock, we gave you room, thinking you needed space," Tiandra replied.

"Then too much time passed," Skyler added. "When we couldn't ping your phone and you didn't answer, we knew something was wrong, so we headed back."

"Figured you'd tried something ridiculous," Graham replied.

"I've got BOLOs out for the sedan, but we don't have much to go off," Walsh said, as though that was news to Chance. "Stay put, let me make some calls."

Chance groaned, running a hand over his head. "How is Marissa doing?"

"She's still in serious condition and unconscious," Tiandra said with a sigh.

The team spouted possible locations in a cacophony of voices until Walsh returned. "State patrol is standing guard over my sister should Sutler or his creeps try another attack."

"Commander, I'm so sorry," Chance said.

"Stop!" Walsh's baritone command silenced the group.

Chance froze. *Here it comes. The termination.* And he'd be forced to sit on the sidelines while the team searched for Ayla. No. He'd find her without their help or approval.

"I'll say this one time, Tavalla, so you'd better listen." Walsh closed the distance between them, his eyes burrowing into Chance like a drill bit. "Casting blame will happen later, but it won't be aimed at you."

Chance stiffened, suddenly returning to basic patrol academy camp with the TAC instructor shouting orders.

Walsh hesitated, then stood, arms folded over his massive chest, feet shoulder width apart. "In this team, we work together, understanding God directs us. You don't get individual glory, and you don't get individual blame. Is that understood?"

Chance fought the urge to look down. His throat tightened. "Yes, sir."

"We will evaluate with a full AAR and debrief when this is over," Walsh said. The after-action report would detail Chance's ginormous blunders and document his termination of employment. Worse, they'd reference it in future training scenarios to demonstrate how Chance had cost three women their lives.

Ayla again came to mind. She'd talked about turning the bad into good. But how could he ever claim such a thing if she died? Guilt slammed into him, reminding Chance he'd focused on himself once more. How did he keep returning to this self-centered place? When had he become such an egomaniac?

"Until then we must focus all our energy on finding Ayla." He placed a hand on Chance's shoulder. "God is in control," Walsh said, ending the discussion.

The kindness nearly unraveled Chance's last thread of composure. The team assembled around him and lowered their voices in prayer. Chance's eyes burned with an unfamiliar sensation. He'd not cried since the day of his childhood gang attack. He would not do that now. "Lord, we need You. Guide our steps and show us how to find Ayla. Protect her, please." The words fell from his lips in vulnerability and honesty.

A collective "Amen" filled the atmosphere, and Chance got a glimpse of his team, all nodding in agreement. Not a condemning expression lingered on their faces. *Lord, thank You for them.* Strobe lights approached, and a fire truck rolled on scene.

"It's a little late now," Chance mumbled.

"They're doing their job," Riker reminded him.

Walsh spoke on the phone, and Chance paced with Destiny beside him. Where would they start? They needed a lead.

Tiandra walked to him. Not wanting to be rude, he refrained from saying he'd like to be alone. Instead, he stood, arms crossed over his chest, standoffish.

"I need to tell you something." Tiandra spoke with authority. Had Walsh sent her?

"Okay." He remained stiff, preparing for the blow.

"Your thoughts are written on your face."

"Ayla said that, too." He averted his gaze. "Then you know I hate myself right now."

"We all share responsibility for what happened here. It's our duty, our drive to protect innocents from being hurt. We took the same oath you did."

Indignation rose within Chance, though his mind ranted to stop. "Except you weren't assigned here. You didn't resent pulling what you saw as the short straw. I didn't want to be her handler. I hated it and even asked Walsh to let someone else take over. You didn't fall in love with her and miss the opportunity to tell her." He sucked in a breath. Had he really confessed that?

Tiandra's expression softened. "If you focus inward, you'll get stuck in that loop of self hatred, and that's a dangerous place to live."

Her words tackled him with the weight of a linebacker at the fifty-yard line.

She was right. He'd swirled into such deep hopelessness, he feared he'd never emerge again.

"Walsh didn't say what he did to cheer you up. He's not like that."

Chance met her eyes. "Really?"

"Has he ever given you the impression he's all about the feels?"

A grin tugged at his lips despite the seriousness. "Not once."

"Exactly. Come on, we need to figure out where Myles Sutler took them."

He trailed behind mutely, and they returned to where the team had assembled at Walsh's SUV. "Sorry." The apology was weak, and he knew it, but nothing else came to mind.

"Been there, dude," Riker said. "Guilt will fog your brain."

"My *abuela* Rios says, don't take any free rides on the guilt train," Skyler said, patting his back.

"I'm trying. I just… I can't stand sitting here and doing nothing."

"We're working on the clues and waiting on information," Skyler reminded him.

"Myles Sutler murdered the judge at his home," Chance said. "Two separate incidents occurred there—"

"Let's get to the Wardens'!" Walsh ordered.

The team slid into their SUVs with Chance and Destiny riding with Riker.

"Should we call for backup?" Skyler asked over the radio.

"No!" Chance said. "If there's an insider working with Sutler, they'll warn him we're on his trail. Surprise is our advantage."

The trip to the house had Chance on edge, and he tapped the dashboard and bounced his leg.

"Dude, you can't go in there wound tighter than a three-day clock," Riker said.

Chance slid back in his seat. "Why did she do that? Beg for my life and take off with him? She knows he'll kill her once he has the list." But Chance knew the answer. She'd traded her life for his.

"Hey, guys, Eliana has something big," Tiandra interrupted. She put her phone on speaker.

"'You'll know George' is an old Haitian saying that means you'll see, or you've got another thing coming," Eliana explained.

"How does that apply to the conversations between Ezra and the unknown party?" Chance asked. "What's the context?"

"It's a blanket warning to Ezra," Tiandra answered.

Chance's mind raced. "That happened days prior to the ambush at the safe house, right? So was the person warning him they were coming?"

"Toward the end of the conversation, it appears so," Tiandra replied.

"Is the other party friend or foe?" Walsh asked.

"That's what I'm wondering," Graham said. "Did the person have something negative on Ezra? Maybe we're talking blackmail or extortion?"

None of this made sense. "But why warn him if you planned to kill him?"

"Nope, we're looking at this wrong," Riker inserted. "What if Ezra had a CI, someone on the inside with Sutler, and he was building the case? They were working together."

"And the warning was that Sutler had made Ezra and the CI," Skyler suggested.

"Exactly," Riker agreed.

"That doesn't explain why Ezra went against protocol. The CI should've been logged into the system," Eliana replied, joining the conversation.

"Unless the CI only agreed to work with Ezra under the radar," Skyler said.

"What advantage does that offer?" Chance asked.

"If that person is on EastSide7's kill list, survival is motive enough," Riker replied. "Knowing the list is filled with corrupt government officials, it's not unwarranted the CI refused to be logged into the system."

"Ezra's got insider knowledge, but he gets too close, and the CI warns Sutler's made them. Ezra tries to get Ayla out of the safe house before they find her when they're ambushed," Chance pieced together.

"There's more," Eliana replied. "Just finished decoding Ezra's files from the cloud. He'd documented the conversations—with none other than Octavia Warden."

"She was the unknown party?" Skyler clarified.

"Yes. She made the mistake of identifying herself in one of the messages," Tiandra chimed in. "Looks like she told him repeatedly that her life was in danger. She refused WitSec."

"Sounds like her," Chance replied.

Eliana continued, "At his recommendation, she stayed away from the Warden house. She promised to help him locate the list."

The line went silent as everyone listened.

Tiandra added, "Ezra was building a case against her."

"Wait, he didn't trust his CI?" Riker asked.

"At first. But as the messages progress, it appears he believed she was working it. She persisted in knowing Ayla's location, which made Ezra suspicious, based on his notes," Eliana explained. "In their last phone call, Octavia offered him a bribe to give up Ayla, and when he declined, she said, 'You'll know George.'"

"He didn't trust Octavia," Walsh added.

Chance asked, "But why claim to have the list?"

"She was working Ezra to find his location. That's how he was compromised," Skyler added.

"Ezra died protecting Ayla," Chance said.

"And since Octavia is working with Sutler, she'll manipulate Ayla by using their family past to gain her trust," Chance said. "She gave an Oscar-worthy performance here as the victim." He slammed his hand on the dash.

"Easy," Riker said. "You're already two for two on damaging vehicles."

"Sorry, man."

"You said Ayla told Myles she'd find the list?" Skyler asked.

"Yeah, but she was just buying time."

"If Ayla doesn't have the list…" Riker began. "He'll figure it out when she keeps stalling."

"And he'll kill her," Chance concluded.

That solidified that the team was walking into a dangerous situation—and Octavia Warden was no innocent party.

In the back seat of the sedan with Octavia, there was little room to move, and Ayla fought the rising panic. Her arms ached from having her wrists bound again.

The ride didn't take as long as Ayla had thought, which gave her hope. Wherever Myles was taking them wasn't far from the Warden home. However, rural land surrounded Iowa in all directions, leaving their location a mystery. Regardless, she prayed for an opportunity to find the list and notify the team before…she swallowed hard…Myles killed her.

Tears welled in her eyes. Why hadn't she told Chance she loved him? She gave a little snort. Right, when should she have done that? While they were escaping the cellar? Or when they'd run for their lives through the pasture while Myles shot at them? Or when he'd caught them? A single droplet slipped down her cheek, and she tasted the saltiness. Still, she should've told him, because now it was too late.

The vehicle stopped, jerking her from her thoughts, and she wondered how long she'd daydreamed of Chance.

Her door opened, warm air wafting in. Myles tugged Ayla from her seat, and she cried out as she stood, weight pressing down on her injured leg. She inhaled deeply, filling her lungs. Sweat trickled down her temples as her eyes adjusted to the dim streetlights. She recognized the pretty garden shed at the far side of the Warden backyard. They were in the alley behind the house, parked at a distance.

Myles dragged Octavia out of the car, too. Her makeup trailed down her face in long black streaks, and her tousled hair hung like a rat's nest.

A dog barked from somewhere nearby, and Ayla wished with all her heart it was Destiny.

Myles poked her in the back with the gun, then gripped her arm and tugged her toward the house. "Open the gate," he ordered Octavia.

She obediently did his bidding, pushing the massive iron gate wide. It creaked in response, and she led them into the backyard. A light illuminated the slate porch.

"There are motion detectors," Octavia explained.

"Stay in the shadows, then," Myles ordered.

His grip on Ayla's arm was cutting off her circulation, but she refused to complain and give him the satisfaction of knowing he'd hurt her.

Once they'd rounded the yard to the house, Myles pointed at Octavia. "You, disarm the alarm. Try anything funny, and I'll make sure Ayla pays for it." He gripped her arm harder.

Octavia nodded. "Okay, but without a key to get in, I'll have to go through the laundry room window. It's small, though—you wouldn't fit. Ayla and I could go through and open the door after I disable the alarm."

A flicker of hope returned. Was Octavia trying to help her escape?

"It doesn't take two people to disable the alarm." Myles nodded toward Ayla. "Besides, she's hurt."

Would Octavia take the opportunity and call the police? Ayla hoped she'd brave it and make the call.

"Remember, she pays for your mistakes," he said, pressing the gun to Ayla's head so hard she winced.

On the other hand, Octavia shouldn't do anything spontaneous.

"I'll just climb through and turn off the alarm."

"You'll know George if you try anything," Myles replied.

Ayla froze at the comment. The same phrase the task force had questioned her about. She willed herself to remain stoic, but her pulse thrummed erratically, and her mind whirled with the implications. Like an annoying splinter under her skin, the words pricked at her with a strange familiarity. Where had she heard it before?

Myles remained with Ayla while Octavia climbed through the window.

The seconds passed like hours as they waited for her return. Maybe she'd called the police after all. Ayla prayed they didn't arrive with lights and sirens, notifying Myles of their presence.

The back door opened, and Octavia waited for them to enter the home. "See? I can follow directions."

"Good to know," Myles mumbled.

Once inside, he stood waiting, with expectation on his face. He gave Ayla control, and she needed to use it to her advantage. Separating from him was the best way to go. They had a better chance of keeping him distracted by going in different directions. He couldn't keep an eye on both of them simultaneously. She had to outsmart him and escape. She had to convince Octavia of the same, because leaving her behind wasn't a choice. Though it was tempting with her constant nagging and complaining. Until she had proof the woman had betrayed her, she refused to believe it.

"All right, Detective Ayla, where do we start?" Myles said.

"Divide and conquer will get us out of here faster," Ayla suggested.

"You're not naive enough to think I'll let you go unsupervised."

"What am I going to do? Run away? Please." Ayla rolled her eyes to emphasize the sarcasm and gestured at her leg. "You've promised we can live and go free once you have the information."

Myles sneered. He'd kill her at the first opportunity. She'd never buy his lies, but he needed to believe otherwise. "Right. Let's go treasure hunting."

"RJ loved gardening. Maybe in the yard? Octavia and I could start in the shed," Ayla said, certain he'd never allow it.

"Um, no. Octavia, you check the shed. Make a run for it, and I'll kill her slowly," Myles warned. "We'll watch and wait."

Octavia nodded and trudged out the door.

He'd trusted her to leave his presence again. The sad confirmation assured Ayla the two were in cahoots. The revelation, though sad, didn't totally surprise Ayla.

Octavia returned minutes later. "Nothing." Fear etched her expression, but Ayla remained suspicious.

"At this rate, we'll be here for days," Ayla said. "Octavia and I will tackle the bedrooms and RJ's study upstairs, while you search the main floor," she told Myles. "You can still monitor us since there's no way out from upstairs."

"Good point."

Octavia led the way. Ayla followed, using the banister to haul herself up the steps. Under her breath she asked, "What does 'you'll know George' mean?"

"What?" Octavia quirked a brow.

"Myles said it earlier."

"Guess I was too scared to notice. Hm, it's an old Haitian saying. My grandmama used to say it to us when we were being naughty. She'd say it as a threat of a spanking."

Ayla latched onto a moment from her childhood when Octavia had come close to spanking her for breaking a vase. *RJ might put up with you, but I'm not as easily conned. You touch one more thing in this house, and you'll know George.* Another memory surfaced of Ezra's phone call that she'd eavesdropped on. *Nothing has changed and no amount of money matters. Are you out of your mind? My job is to protect her!* By Octavia's own admission, she or Myles had tried bribing Ezra.

The familiar stab of betrayal hit Ayla, but she couldn't allow her emotions to show. She had to notify the task force of her location, and fast. "Look in your bedroom. Maybe there's a hidden box?"

Octavia's eyes widened. "Good idea."

Ayla entered RJ's study and moved to his massive mahogany desk, where she retrieved his iPad mini hidden in the bottom drawer. Had Myles not looked for it? Or did he assume RJ used the laptop? She connected the charging cord and plugged it into the outlet, keeping one eye on the door as the device powered on slowly.

She swiped the screen and entered his password, familiar with it since he used the same one for his office, too. He'd trusted her with everything. Perhaps as penance for accepting her father's bribe. Though he'd probably done so to protect her and her family. Regardless, it was wrong, and she wouldn't pretend otherwise. With one last glimpse at the door, Ayla leaned forward and quickly tapped the internet browser to open RJ's email. Send help. I'm at the Warden house with Octavia and Myles Sut—

A slam from behind snapped Ayla's neck forward. "I wouldn't send that if I were you." Octavia stood with a scowl on her face.

"Now, see, we thought you were smarter than that," Myles said, stepping into the room.

"All this time, you were working together?" Ayla asked, stumbling back into the bookshelves.

"RJ said you were brilliant, but I can't say I agree," Octavia said. "Stop playing games. Where's the list?"

Ayla visually surveyed the room, spotting the old shotgun RJ had called "The Enforcer" propped in the corner. She averted her eyes. Why was it in here? RJ always secured the weapon in his basement gun safe. *Please, Lord, let it be loaded.*

Octavia inched forward, forcing Ayla to move to the side. RJ's sterling silver letter opener sat perched on the edge of the desk. Forcing away the pain, Ayla prayed for courage.

"Okay, you win." She looked down, thrust the iPad at Octavia, striking her in the face, and lunged across the desk. Ayla snagged the letter opener and skidded off the desk to the other side. She landed in a squat, then bolted for the gun.

THIRTEEN

Walsh spoke over the radio as they pulled into the alley behind the Warden home. "Go dark. Park on the back side. Dogs enter first and approach from the rear. Do not draw attention to yourselves."

A series of replies filled the line with, "Roger that."

"Got it."

"Affirmative."

Then radio silence in obedience to Walsh's orders to eliminate any communication channels.

Chance exited Riker's vehicle and paused. Each member donned their Kevlar vests and added extra magazines to their tactical belts, providing additional firepower. Riker tossed him an extra set he kept on hand.

In silent formation, the team crept along the fence line.

Chance noticed a sedan parked a distance away and partially hidden by a large dumpster. He motioned toward it, and the team paused as he offered Destiny Ayla's scent article from his pocket. He then gave her the hand commands for *silent* and *seek*. Together, they made their way to the car.

Destiny alerted at the driver's side passenger door. Chance gave an affirmative nod, and they moved back into formation, approaching the open garden gate.

Chance and Destiny took the lead toward the darkened

house. Riker and Ammo stayed behind him, Tiandra and Bosco aimed for the gardening shed, while Walsh and Skyler moved for the front door and side windows. Chance and Destiny went for the back door.

A gunshot from the house stopped the team. Each searched for the shooter, followed by head shakes. The sound had come from inside the home.

Chance stepped forward, and Riker pressed a hand to his shoulder. He turned, and Riker held up a window punch. With a nod, Chance took the tool and used it to break out the glass on the country-style six-window panel door. He reached inside and turned the knob.

They entered in stealth mode.

Voices above in contentious tones drew him toward the stairs. Riker and Ammo stayed close behind, the rest of the team entering and spreading out to cover the exits. He gave Destiny the hand commands for *silent*. With Riker's confirming touch on his shoulder, they ascended the stairs.

Ayla stood motionless. Myles had fired at her, thankfully missing. She was close to the shotgun.

"Someone's here," Octavia said, slamming the door.

Myles twisted to look at her. "Hold them off!"

That was all the diversion Ayla needed. She plunged the letter opener into his thigh. He screamed and struck her forehead with the gun. She stumbled to the side, clutching her face, warm with fresh blood. Ayla sucked in a fortifying breath and dived for The Enforcer, her fingertips grazing the weapon just as Octavia screamed and tackled her.

Ayla used her good leg to kick free, striking Octavia twice in the face. She released her hold, allowing Ayla to crawl forward and grasp the shotgun.

She clamped down with a death grip on the weapon and rolled onto her back. With the shotgun positioned in front of her, she moved backward, getting to her feet as Myles and Octavia stood dumbfounded. Over Octavia's shoulder, Ayla spotted the door slowly opening.

"Put it down," Myles ordered. His carotid artery pulsed, animating the ugly tattoo there.

Ayla positioned her finger on the trigger.

"You won't shoot." He lunged for her, and Ayla pulled the trigger.

Nothing happened. Confused, she glanced down.

Myles closed the distance.

Ayla gripped the shotgun and swung it like a baseball bat, knocking him off balance.

Octavia rushed at her, and they tumbled to the floor.

"US Marshals!"

"Drop your weapons!"

The team flooded the room, but Ayla fixed her gaze on Myles holding a Bowie knife, ready to plunge it into her heart.

He lifted his arm with a murderous glare.

A blur of brown and black blazed behind him, tackling Myles. He hollered, and Ayla got to her feet.

Ayla blinked twice, confused at the sight of Destiny with her jaws clamped onto Myles's arm. The Bowie knife lay on the floor near Octavia. Both women dived for it, but Ayla succeeded, jerking the weapon out of reach.

"Get down!" Riker hollered, his gun aimed at Octavia.

She stilled, dropping to her knees, and lifted her hands in surrender. "Ignorant girl!" she spat at Ayla.

Chance entered the room.

Ayla sucked in a breath, hardly able to believe her eyes. No.

It couldn't be him.

He'd died in the bomb explosion. Ayla blinked, desperate to hold onto the sight of him while needing to get a grasp on reality.

It was her mind, playing tricks on her.

Had to be.

"Ayla," Chance spoke her name and, in an instant, her knees buckled, and she clung to the chair for support.

"Chance," she whispered, still unable to move.

"Time to go." Tiandra took custody of Octavia, snapping cuffs on her wrists as she spewed hateful words at Ayla.

"Destiny, release!" Chance commanded again, reverting Ayla's attention to where the shepherd held on, shaking her head, mouth clamped down on Myles's forearm.

He writhed and fought, trying to strike her with his unimpeded fist and missing every time.

"If you keep fighting, she won't let go," Chance ordered.

Myles relented, unmoving, his face twisted in a grimace.

Chance stepped closer. "Destiny, release."

Reluctantly, she obeyed, growling with bared teeth as she retreated in a slow backward stalk.

Myles cradled his arm. "She broke my arm," he whined.

Riker took custody, dragging Myles to his feet. "Don't worry, you'll have plenty of time to tell your sad story in prison."

"Two thirty-eight–PSI bite capacity," Chance said with a grin. "Good girl, Destiny!" She wagged her tail as he ruffled her fur, praising her efforts. He withdrew a stuffed shark and tossed it to the dog, and she chomped down, enjoying the toy. Chance met Ayla's gaze and crossed the room.

Ayla ignored the pain in her leg and threw herself into his waiting arms.

"Are you okay?" he asked her.

"Yes." Her body shook with the adrenaline rush. "But how's it possible? Myles said he set a bomb in the SUV. I heard it."

"He did. Destiny alerted, and thanks to you, we escaped just in time." He gestured to Riker. "Get paramedics here for Ayla's leg, please."

"On it." His teammate dragged Myles from the room.

"Thank You, Lord!" She clung to Chance, her leg throbbing with her heartbeat. Ayla didn't care. Chance was alive.

"Yes, God had everything to do with it." He grinned mischievously.

"How did you know we'd be here?" Ayla asked.

"It's a long story." Chance drew her closer, and in her peripheral, she noticed the rest of the team exiting the room. "Whew, I thought they'd never leave."

She chuckled.

"I've never been more afraid or desperate in my life. When he kidnapped you and we couldn't find you, I felt like everything I thought mattered was suddenly worthless."

Ayla looked down, tears welling. "Chance, I need to tell you something."

"Wait, please let me say this before I implode."

"Okay."

He stepped back, perching on the end of RJ's desk, and took her hands into his. "Ayla, I owe you an apology."

"Whatever for?"

"When Walsh assigned your protection detail to me, I wanted to refuse, not because of you, but because of my own insecurities. Then, every attack and finally your abduction just added to that."

"You did everything to protect me. I'm the one who foolishly went off with who I thought was a firefighter. That's not on you."

"It is, but I know now placing blame won't help. When you were gone, I realized nothing else matters. I am in love with you, Ayla DuPree."

She blinked. "You are?"

He nodded. "I was always attracted to you. But I cast my disdain for RJ Warden onto you. That wasn't right."

"Yeah, but you were right about RJ." Ayla glanced down.

"He made a mistake once a long time ago, but it doesn't mean that's something he continued to do," Chance said.

Ayla looked at him. "Is that why he was so close to my family? Out of obligation or penance?"

"Maybe both, but not in a bad way. He cared for your family. RJ made a poor choice, but that doesn't make him a bad person. He sinned, like we all do. He tried to make the right choices by refusing the bribe from Myles Sutler, and he gave his life for it."

Ayla's eyes filled with tears. "You're right. Thank you. Okay, my turn?"

Chance inhaled deeply. "Hit me."

She chuckled. "When I was in the cellar, all I could think was how much I regretted not telling you how I felt about you, too. I mean, you're gorgeous, but I can look beyond that," she teased.

"I'm glad to hear it." He laughed.

"You're an amazing man. I might've fallen for you when I captured you and Destiny in the fishing net."

Destiny glanced up with a whine.

"Sorry about that, sweetie." Ayla snickered. "Or maybe it was when you told me to keep the gun I found at the cabin. I'm not sure when it happened, but what I feel for you is real."

"I've waited too long to do this." Chance glanced down, his hooded eyes soaking her in as he leaned forward. Ayla lifted her head, pressing closer until their lips met. The kiss deepened, absorbing the lost time, the terrifying moments and the desperation they'd experienced. It lasted longer than Ayla expected and ended before she was ready.

Someone cleared his throat in the background, interrupting the moment. With reluctance, Ayla stepped back, pressing her fingers against her lips to hold the kiss close. She peered around Chance's muscled chest to where Riker stood. "Sorry, but I promise you two will want to hear what Sutler's got to say."

They trailed him to the living room, where blue and red lights flashed through the windows. Sutler sat clinging to his arm. "EastSide7 will kill me. You must let me go."

"Don't waste our time," Walsh said.

"Fine, but you don't understand. If you don't protect me, they'll come after me. With or without the list. I'll tell you whatever you want to know, but you have to protect me," Myles bargained.

"What can you offer?" Walsh asked, his arms crossed, feet shoulder width apart, looking menacing and large.

"I can tell Ayla why Octavia betrayed her and give you what you need to take down EastSide7 for good."

"Why would we believe you?" Riker asked.

Myles blinked. "Because if you don't, they'll kill me. I have nothing left. The last time you arrested me, they warned I'd die if I didn't find the list. For real, man, you gotta help me."

"If you produce anything worth following up on, I'll talk to the DA." Walsh glanced at Riker, who nudged Myles. He struggled to his feet, clutching his arm.

"Okay, spill," Chance told him, holding Ayla close.

"Shortly before his death, RJ suspected my relationship with Octavia. We didn't mean for it to happen. But we're from the same hometown and we have common connections. Octavia's worked hard to hide her past and she denied the affair to RJ, but he didn't believe her," Myles said. "He revised his will, leaving everything to Ayla. She was furious, but with her connections, managed to hide the new will."

Ayla's mouth hung agape.

"Let me get this straight—Ayla is RJ's heir?" Chance clarified.

"Yes. See? I'll help you if you'll protect me."

"We'll see what we can do," Walsh replied. "Get him out of here."

"With pleasure." Skyler and Graham escorted Myles out.

"Commander Walsh, is Marissa okay?" Ayla asked.

His lips turned downward. "She's stable but still unconscious."

Ayla's eyes welled. "I'm so sorry."

Walsh placed a hand on her shoulder. "The only person who needs to apologize just left with a broken arm," he said. "You did a great job of helping us find you."

Ayla thanked him, but when the paramedics rushed inside, Chance cut her off. "Here. She's got a gunshot wound." Chance led them to her, then moved protectively beside her. "I want to hear everything that happened prior to our arrival."

Ayla shared the events and how she'd pieced together that Octavia was working with Myles. "I didn't want to believe it, but with Myles's confession, I guess it makes sense."

"I understand," Chance said, kneeling in front of her.

"You're going to need stitches, but it's a through and through GSW," the paramedic announced. "Let's get you loaded into the rig."

Ayla shook her head. "I'll ride with Chance and Destiny."

"Okay." The medic rose and exited the room.

Chance helped her up, placing a hand at the small of her back. "That was incredibly risky and wrong."

"What?"

"Leaving me in the dog kennel and leading Myles Sutler back here."

Ayla shrugged. "I didn't have a fishing net on hand."

Chance laughed and kissed her again. "You're incorrigible."

"Thank you." She tried to curtsy and teetered. "If I could've fired The Enforcer, the whole showdown would've ended sooner."

"The what?" Chance quirked a brow.

"Upstairs. The shotgun." She turned.

"Stay here. I'll get it." He ran up the stairs, returning seconds later with the shotgun.

"I'll show you." She reached for it.

"Whoa, slow down with a loaded weapon," Riker said.

"That's just it. It's not loaded." She opened the loading port. "What's this?" In place of a shotgun shell, cotton filled the space. Ayla extracted it, and a small black jump drive fell onto the floor. She looked up, meeting Chance's wide eyes. "The list?"

"Possibly." Riker lifted the object. "I'll get it to Tiandra. Stand by." He hurried from the room.

Chance took Ayla's hand in his. "Can I say it again?" he asked.

"What?"

"I love you."

"Oh, yes, please say that as many times as you want." She rose to her tiptoes and met him in a delicious kiss.

"Sorry to interrupt," Riker said.

They parted, and she glanced down, her cheeks coloring from getting caught again by the same team member.

"Then stop doing it," Chance teased.

"The drive has the list!" Riker and Chance high-fived.

Walsh entered. "I heard. Great job."

"I'm free?" Ayla asked.

"No." Walsh shook his head.

"Does this mean I go back into WitSec?" Ayla asked, fearing the answer.

"That might be the best option for now. Until we've gone through whatever is on that drive, we still have a lot of criminals unaccounted for. You're not safe until we're done arresting the parties involved," Walsh said with a sad smile. "That's probably not what you want to hear."

"No, but I understand." She met Chance's eyes. What did that mean for them? How did you start a relationship with someone under witness protection?

"Whatever it means, I'm not going anywhere without you. I'd marry you today just to join you," Chance said.

Ayla slid her arms around his neck. "And I'd say yes." She kissed him, not caring who saw this time, relishing his touch. "But it's not feasible. You're needed."

"I'm sorry to eavesdrop, but you're right, Ayla," Walsh said. "Chance and Destiny are top fugitive trackers, and until we take down every EastSide7 member and the corrupt individuals working with them, you're not safe."

Chance held her close. "Will you wait for me?"

"As long as it takes," she promised.

"If the number is as big as Sutler's saying, we'll have serious housecleaning to do."

"Yep, and it'll be a full-time job arresting all these people," Riker said.

"Don't plan any vacation time," Walsh said, slapping Chance on the back.

"Told you so," Riker replied under his breath. "Come

on, boss. Let's leave these two alone for a few minutes."
He ushered Walsh from the room.

The moment was bittersweet. They'd arrested Octavia and Myles and hopefully found what they needed to take down the rest of the corruption involved with EastSide7. But how long would it take to end her nightmare?

"Are you okay with long engagements?" Chance asked.

Her eyes welled with tears. "Yes."

"Be ready with your dress, Ayla DuPree. Because when we arrest the last criminal, I'm marrying you."

"Count on it," she said, kissing him again.

EPILOGUE

Six months later

Chance leaned on the split rail fence, and Destiny nudged his hand with a whine. He stroked her soft fur in a silent communication of support. Ammo and Bosco rushed ahead, sniffing the grounds, while Destiny remained close. She hadn't left his side since they'd rescued Ayla.

"I understand why Ayla had to go into WitSec and why I couldn't be her handler," Chance explained to his K-9 companion. "But that doesn't help me miss her less."

Tiandra and Eliana had extracted all the information from the jump drive where RJ Warden had not only kept the list but also detailed records documenting the individuals, transgressions, payments and dates. Everything the team needed to take down the corrupt parties involved. Additionally, Warden had bequeathed all his possessions and money to Ayla. Octavia had set her eyes on destroying Ayla and tried hiding the information.

The man Chance had deemed a crook had worked to take down EastSide7. And the first opportunity he got, he'd tell Ayla how right she was to love RJ. He'd made mistakes by taking the bribe for her father. There was no sugarcoating that truth. But he'd done some good, too.

Once Ayla learned about her sudden inheritance, she worked with the district attorney to get the embezzled money returned. Maybe RJ had died compiling the list as a way of atoning for his sins. They might never know.

Most shocking were the familiar names of government officials and criminal justice personnel in all levels listed on the file. EastSide7 had done their due diligence to ensure their corruption reached all necessary parties, keeping their crooks out of prison. That same list ensured the Heartland Fugitive Task Force arrested every person. Additionally, Sutler's gun was compared against the ballistics evidence extracted from George, the gelatin mannequin, confirming him and several other EastSide7 members as shooters on Gavin's Point Dam.

Last night, Riker and Chance had celebrated the last arrest. He couldn't wait to get to Ayla.

Destiny strolled beside Chance as they surveyed the Walsh property. The horses had returned, and they meandered around the pasture, their tails swishing flies. Walsh had called a team meeting here. Chance hoped it was brief.

Walsh strode toward him, and Chance smiled. The commander had assured him there would be no repercussions for his actions, and he no longer feared losing his job. He'd learned his lesson in the importance of following protocol. They'd completed the after-action report, classifying Chance's mistakes as lessons learned.

The barn was in a state of repair, though the sight of it was still a painful visual reminder of the events. Though Walsh had assured him their insurance would cover the repair costs, regret filled Chance at the sight of the damage. Once more, he thanked God that no one, including the horses, had perished in the fire. And added gratitude for Marissa's recovery. "Lord, You amaze me with Your ways. Thank You for helping us get to Ayla. You get it, right?"

Destiny met his eyes with compassion and love.

"Destiny, why didn't I keep you with us? You'd have protected Ayla even when I failed." A wet nuzzle of reassurance said his shepherd had forgiven him.

Ammo and Bosco ran by, and Chance turned to see Tiandra and Riker waving him back to the house. The roar of an engine approached.

Skyler's SUV. She must have an update for them. Chance and Destiny jogged to meet her, catching up with Riker, Walsh and Tiandra at the vehicle.

Unable to see through the dark-tinted windows, Chance stood to the side.

The passenger door opened, and white fabric flowed out.

Ayla emerged wearing a stunning wedding dress, her auburn hair pinned up with tendrils framing her face. She'd never looked more beautiful.

He gasped. "What're you doing here?"

"It's good to see you, too!" She laughed as he lifted her into the air and kissed her full on the lips.

Walsh cleared his throat, and Chance slowly set Ayla down on her feet.

Marissa exited the rear passenger seat and stood beside her brother. "This is my kind of happy ending."

"I feel like I missed a big email notification," Chance said.

"We wanted to surprise you," Ayla said. "My mom and Boyd will be joining us later this afternoon, so I'll finally get a chance to introduce you."

"That's awesome! Does this mean you're free from WitSec?" Chance asked Ayla, though his focus remained on Walsh.

"Yes, it does," Walsh replied. "Ayla is no longer in hiding."

Chance whooped and hollered, lifting Ayla into his

arms and swinging her around. He kissed her then ran to his SUV, gathering the ring from his duffel bag where it had waited for this moment the past months. He sprinted to Ayla, his team standing by, wide-eyed. But a knowing look hovered in Marissa's blue eyes since she'd helped him pick out the ring. She winked.

Chance dropped to one knee with the ring extended. "Ayla DuPree, would you marry me?"

Ayla glanced at the group, a finger poised on her chin. "Hmm…" A pause hung in the air.

"You already have the dress," Skyler teased.

"True, but that's because Chance asked me to have one ready when you all closed the EastSide7 case," Ayla replied, glancing down as if seeing the white flowing fabric for the first time.

"Please?" Chance whispered.

Ayla smiled. "Of course!"

Chance slid the ring on her finger, then rose and pulled her into his arms, promising he'd never again let her go.

* * * * *

COMING NEXT MONTH FROM
Love Inspired Suspense

COLD CASE REVENGE
Pacific Northwest K-9 Unit • by Jessica R. Patch
When Nick Rossi's three-year-old daughter disappears, it's up to Special Agent Ruby Orton and her K-9 to find her. But once they locate the child, it's an eerie echo of a decades-old case involving Nick's sister. And someone's killing to keep the past a secret...

AMISH COUNTRY RANSOM
by Mary Alford
FBI agent Jade Powell is sent on a twisted journey through Amish country when an enemy from her past abducts her sister. Now she must rely on K-9 trainer Ethan Connors to survive the mountains, the coming storm and a deadly weapons smuggler who will do anything to remain hidden.

MOUNTAIN ABDUCTION RESCUE
Crisis Rescue Team • by Darlene L. Turner
When her son is kidnapped by a serial arsonist out for revenge, park warden Hazel Hoyt must team up with firefighter Mitchell Booth to track down her missing child. But with danger closing in on all sides, can they survive long enough to save her son?

BIG SKY SECRETS
by Amity Steffen
After his ex drops off his surprise toddler son, then turns up dead, rancher Eric Montgomery enlists the help of a former family friend. Will private investigator Cassie Anderson be able to untangle the lethal mysteries tied to Eric's past before he becomes the next victim?

WYOMING RANCH AMBUSH
by Sommer Smith
Evie Langford's move to Wyoming is meant to be a fresh start...until her ex-boyfriend's death makes her the target of a kingpin. Accused of having money stolen from the crime boss, Evie needs cowboy Beau Thorpe's protection before she pays for a crime she didn't commit.

HUNTING THE WITNESS
by Kate Angelo
After interrupting a kidnapping, scientist Belinda Lewis becomes the key witness in a high-profile crime—and the evidence she has points to FBI agent Jonah Phillips. But when Jonah saves her life during an attack, Belinda can't remember who she is...let alone why she's now caught in the crosshairs of a killer.

LOOK FOR THESE AND OTHER LOVE INSPIRED BOOKS WHEREVER BOOKS ARE SOLD, INCLUDING MOST BOOKSTORES, SUPERMARKETS, DISCOUNT STORES AND DRUGSTORES.

LISCNM0723

HARLEQUIN
PLUS

Try the best multimedia subscription service for romance readers like you!

Read, Watch and Play.

Experience the easiest way to get the romance content you crave.

Start your **FREE TRIAL** at
<u>www.harlequinplus.com/freetrial</u>.